Readers LOVE '

"I saved The Return Present for my holiday treat read and wow!! I can honestly say I was truly blown away, what an amazing debut book. Gorgeous, lyrical, poetic text, the story had me rapt, I didn't want it to end. Think Vikram Seth meets Arundhati Roy but still with Lakshman's own unique style. A fabulous read and one that will stay with me for a while."

"Amazing. Not generally given to writing reviews but this one needs to be written about. Truly captivating writing…a rich and beautiful piece of work"

"I absolutely loved this story about strong, determined and still feminine women!"

"Absolutely loved this book … could barely put it down. Plenty of laugh out loud moments amongst all the intrigue and drama. A beautifully written page turner!"

"A little jewel of a book about everything that matters. The most human of stories, shot through with the laugh-out-loud."

"Deeply poignant, joyously spirited, superbly written. Pure gold!"

"Something special has come our way. An emotional rollercoaster!"

"Funny as well as well as heart-wrenching. A good book club read!"

"What a wonderful book. I found it impossible to put down. It was so beautifully written. It made me laugh out loud and cry a few times, the characters felt so alive. Was sad that it had to end."

THE
RETURN PRESENT

Sonia Lakshman

For my beloved family
For Roshie
And for the cosmos

PROLOGUE

LATER

She flew northward into the thickening dark, wings beating silently, high, high above the icy air. Her black feathers glistened, each fibril alive with the wind, tips lifting in an instinctive orchestration of a complexity so intricate, that to fathom it would take many a fine mind into chasms of unknowable wonder. She caught the current. Her beak pierced the way ahead, a ship's sharp masthead spearing through the cold, cutting, splicing through virgin height, as the sky gave way to her - or if you look closer - *for* her perhaps. The airy throng curtsied for Majesty, glad and honoured to have been so close, pushing and parting, to get closer to her still. All so the winds could say - when she had vanished at a speed so fast that you scarce knew she had been there - that they had been pressed against the actual inky velvet, that was the great raven Kalina. She banked. Her wings spread wide over the land and night fell.

Far below, so far that if you dropped a pebble it would burrow a crater as wide as ten miles just with its impact - so let's be careful not to drop anything lest whole populations be obliterated overnight without reason, populations that never saw it coming, never knew that this was their last supper, would have made it more special had they known, the way we make things special only once we've lost them or are about to or someone else does, until we forget again– far below in the crimson city crisscrossed with dusty lanes, a frail, steely lady wipes her forehead with the fraying cotton edge of her sari. Beads of sweat gather above her eyebrows, a singular droplet precariously overhanging as if dangling from a cliff. She is sat on the edge of the charpoy bed, her frame so slight that the bed strings hardly bow with her weight that isn't weight - bird-like, wafer thin skin, wrapping wafer white bone. She holds the water in her mouth, careful not to swallow. She must not swallow. She *will not* swallow. Her eyes harden in determination and in that tightening a soft, salty, tear escapes, slipping down her cheek and coming to rest in the dry shelf of her lower lip. She must not lick it, she *will not* lick it, no water will pass her lips.

All her life Ferangiz had been right. She had been right about Mehnaz's marriage, about exactly how much salt is needed to correctly sweeten aubergine, about the name of the black bird with the yellow beak – no it is not a koel, it is a myna – about Farida's blood pressure, her systoles and diastoles, she'd been right about her students results, who would pass, who would fail (none of Ferangiz's students fail), about where the keys were, everyone always asked Ferangiz where the keys were, because Ferangiz always knew and Ferangiz was always right.

2

It was important she felt to be able to predict things. Where are we without order? Science is order. Mathematics is order. Let's ignore the discombobulating presence of black holes for now because we don't want to look too closely at anything that might upset the tight equilibrium. She'd turn her righteous head the other way and set about neatening the desk where the red pens were out of line. Anything she passes she adjusts, corrects, neatens, straightens, pats down, pulls up. She adjusts the tie of a wayward pupil. 'Like this, child. A double knot, always a double knot' – unravelling the worn-shiny blue cotton and tying it again sure and practiced – and the child flushed with a sort of pleasure, because despite her sternness there was something about Ferangiz that made any attention from her, even her reprimands, somehow prized. You only got it if she thought you were worth it. And if Ferangiz thought you were worth it, you were. Everyone wanted to please her. But Ferangiz as we know, is not a woman to be easily pleased.

And now for the first time she was wrong.

Part One

MEHNAZ

CHAPTER 1

Many a time Mehnaz wondered what would have happened to Ferangiz if Homi Uncle hadn't died. She would get back home from the dusty day and see her sat on the long verandah, frowning through her thick spectacles at her students' essays, scratching at them with her red pen, the pile of exercise books gathering higher to her right as she scathed them one at a time, never looking up, not pausing, not even once. Mehnaz would catch her from a distance, from where Ferangiz looked oddly vulnerable the way she never did up close, an isolated figure who had made herself unreachable, like a lone star in a spinning galaxy. We are all made for contact, thought Mehnaz. Skin to skin, cheek to cheek, cheek by jowl, we jostle through life together, sweat and feelings and thoughts and dreams entangled, and though we might try and unthread ourselves from each other, when we do we are scattered islands, once more longing for the thronging continent and its anchor and caress. If there was ever a creature made for contact it was Mehnaz herself, for to be with her was to want to touch her. And not just everyone around her: dogs nuzzled, cats rubbed up, honeysuckle tendrils reached, sheets purred, seats greeted her – but wait, we stray.

She was the only one who could touch Ferangiz. Let's be clear, this is the subtlest of contact, mind. Not hugs. Not sloppy embrace. No squeezes. Bringing her tea, made just the way Mehnaz knows she likes it, in the right cup, with the right saucer and the right spoon, the water not boiled to bubbling, nor tepid, just under, the tea leaves orange pekoe in the morning peeking out with the orange sun, a thin tisane in the evening the thin grey colour of dusk. She sets it down for her on the little table with the old white doily, neatly pressed, no creases, then pours it. No milk. And in the handing, Ferangiz, or as Mehnaz calls her, Izzy Aunty – no one else is allowed to call her that only her niece, though this has never been stated, is implicit like an inheritance, except Mehnaz has earned it, without ever trying, she's earned it, the way the others without ever trying have lost it, like a careless spend or an unthinking roll of the dice – she looks up ever so slightly and in that handing of the cup and then the departing, Mehnaz's hand would touch hers. Less than a touch, a feather brush, less than a feather brush, a breeze, less than a breeze, a breath…a filigree breath of light fingers on skin. But Mehnaz knew and so did Izzy Aunty, though Izzy Aunty would never admit it, exactly what that meant.

Is it possible to feel tenderness and pride in the same moment, is it possible to feel that softest of feelings together with this bristling one? It seems it is, for that was exactly the feeling that would flutter and bristle in Mehnaz's breast, every time. She left the verandah. Neither had said a word. But this was all before, before all that was to come.

CHAPTER 2

Mehnaz sat outside on the crumbling step. While her world jostled around her – Farida calling out to Hema to hurry with the hot water, Raju sweeping outside, all but disappearing in a dusty eddy himself, so much so that it was possible to believe that there was a diminutive tornado appeared in their yard all the way from Kansas, his dust-reddened chappals sticking out the bottom like an Indian Dorothy, Shanaz pretending to hummingly study her algebra while lost in an altogether more ephemeral equation, Almaz chattering into the phone thirty to the dozen – Mehnaz sat outside on the crumbling step looking out on the old orchard in the setting sun, wondering how she would ever leave it all. The time was coming and it seemed the whole household was speeding up in an ever-accelerating flurry, as if by some twist of time travel if they moved fast enough it wouldn't happen or they wouldn't notice it happening and they would never know that their beloved Mehnaz was going, going, gone, the whole household, a scurrying hurricane denying the prospect of their treasured jewel being lifted up and carried away.

Mehnaz sat in the eye of it. As much as they sped up, she slowed down. Where normally she would bustle through the house, her sunny voice lighting up even the dustiest of corners, high notes finding their way to the tops of the cupboards, low trebles settling under the beds, stray notes cascading into the parts Hema with her lazy feather duster often missed, the whole house lilting as she cajoled and caroused, bringing them all together despite themselves – now, as if weighed by the pressure of departure, not unlike the heaviness of an imminent thunderstorm, she sat. She sat still. Maybe if she didn't move, maybe if she didn't breathe, maybe it would all stay the same. The clouds wouldn't break. Everything would be how it had always been and how it always would be.

It wasn't like she wasn't longing for the deluge. For the swamping of his kiss. It wasn't like she didn't always feel slightly giddy of late, slightly unsteady on her feet, her fingers unconsciously touching her own lips as though to insinuate his presence. It wasn't as if she didn't feel a near constant moistening between her rose plump thighs. It was hardly as though she didn't arch in bed alone at night in a way that she hoped no one saw. It would be unfair to assume that her breasts were not just a little more generous as they rose and swelled towards his imagined touch. It was all she could do to not too obviously lean over tabletops just grazing herself against their corners, or to squirm a little too vigorously in the tickly rattan chair, the stray threads pleasingly scratchy if she angled herself just right. Her young body had been awoken by his arrival, by his strange maleness, and now it was curled in a constant state of almost unbearable anticipatory ecstasy as the prospect of him grew closer and closer. All of nature gathered in her and then flowered in a near obscene pheromonal concoction that was enough to drive any male passing downwind to irreparable distraction. She was a vol-cano, a Venus about to pop.

And yet, she was still. Coupled with this flood of longing was the old summer, a rift valley in her midst. She couldn't bear that she would have to leave her home for him. She sat, trying to hold the two worlds without moving. Maybe if I sit very still, if I sit very, very still she thought, it will all come to rest at my feet. Maybe I will never have to leave. Maybe by some kind of grace, Manoj will be moved here to Poona and I will never have to walk out of the gate away from here. The thought of it, of that moment of departure, a plunging tunnel that her mind darkly flew down, made all her longing drop from her and an icy chill, a chill that clawed around her heart and contracted her soft, warm being into a fragile shard that the slightest touch might shatter.

'Didi!' come for dinner, Almaz yelled to her sister. The shard melted, a sudden spring. She was still here, she had not left, the gates hadn't clanged behind her, and Mehnaz rejoiced in the temporary reprieve. 'Arre, Hema Maushi, you made my paneer,' she said joyfully to the cook who'd been with them before Mehnaz had been born and before that and before that, as she stuck her fingers into the dish on its way to the dining table, her appetites suddenly returning just as quickly as they'd vanished. Hema beamed, the goitre sticking out of her neck a bit more. There was no way she would have allowed anyone else to taste anything ahead, let alone stick their fingers in it and help themselves enroute. Hema patted her goitre with pleasure. Not even she was immune.

The household gathered to eat. Here was the order of seating. Almaz perpetually starving was always first. Farida, fussing over her daughters sat next to her, the chair opposite her empty for Mehnaz who herded Shanaz in from wherever she was absently drifting about the house, seemingly oblivious of the need to eat or of the need for everyone else to. Ferangiz sat at the head and came in last. This was not as autocratic as it might seem. She simply could not bear to wait for the family to settle and had over the years perfected her timing such that she entered just as Shanaz was finally found. For those with a sensitive eye they might notice that Ferangiz's entry this evening was ever so slightly cold, and that when she sat down, she did so with a tautness beyond her customary upright carriage. Farida, seemed to fuss a little more over the girls than usual, neither woman looking at the other. Hema thumped in and out, bringing in fresh rotis hot off the tawa, Almaz ate them faster than usual, Mehnaz passing them round with a slightly worried frown. Only Shanaz was unchanged, as oblivious as ever to the world outside her own head.

So, you might ask, what exactly is going on here?

Digging swiftly a little deeper you might say *why* is this girl leaving her beloved shore? Why are they letting her go? Why are they all subjecting themselves to heartbreak in this way? Who is this Manoj and why has everyone agreed to this? And these would be very, very good questions indeed. Questions that Ferangiz wanted her sister Farida to answer, or to put that more accurately, questions that Farida had not answered but that hung in the air like an angry shroud.

Here are the facts. In a household of all women – barring Raju who sweeps the yard, who we will not include in this count because he is simply here to sweep the yard, shoo the birds, close the gates, bring in the post, sell the old newspapers, collect the milk from the clanking can by the buffalo and do anything else of Hema's bidding, though not fast enough for Hema's liking in a way that makes her goitre swell with annoyance when her eyes fall on his dawdling form – in a household of all women in an India of a certain time, a young unmarried woman is as much a liability as anything else. Not that anyone in the household thought of Mehnaz in these terms, we know that. We don't need to elaborate on that or on the love that encases and billows around her, like the satiny jeweller's case in which sits a ruby. The irony was it was *because* of this that Farida felt it was her responsibility to get her daughter settled, settled well and settled fast. It was *because* she treasured her daughter that she took it upon her shoulders to get her out of this house of women, even out of this faith that had so let her down – ex communication be damned – to break the curse that seemed, in her opinion, to befall them, to have her spoken for and to do so quickly. No, her mother thought, Mehnaz for all her allure – perhaps like all truly alluring people she seemed entirely unaware of her charms – could not be left or trusted to do this by herself. Ferangiz apparently disagreed. Still, Ferangiz could rule the roost on everything else in the house, have the last word on every other debate, preside over every other decision, but this decision, this decision would be hers. On that Farida was clear. Mehnaz was her daughter. *Hers.*

CHAPTER 3

Farida had not intended it to happen quite as quickly as it did, nor in the way it did, nor with whom it did. She had set the ball in motion quite innocuously just mentioning it in passing to her friend Bina who was visiting from Delhi as they sat drinking tea in the afternoon, just mentioning that she would be so happy if her Mehnaz would get settled soon, did not have to be a Parsi boy, just a nice boy. She swore to Ferangiz later, much later, when the thunder finally broke, that

that was all she had said. But as someone once postulated, an elephant's fart in Africa – or maybe it was a butterfly's wing in Brazil – can set off a typhoon in Asia, all things being irreparably interconnected with a habit of domino-ing more often than fizzling out. And so it was that the casual utterance from Farida's lips as she lifted the cup to them that afternoon, made its way to the vibrating tympanum of Bina's middle ear and thence by a convoluted passage of biology and synaptic activity out of Bina's mouth, dropping seemingly casually into the conversations in the lounge room down a leafy street in Delhi, where so happened to live Mrs. Diwan, who so happened to know Mrs. Prabhakar, who so happened to have a son of very marriageable age, and was looking for just such a girl from just such an old family, even if this family had come upon tough times and their wealth was no longer what it had once been, maybe even crumbling, this was not the point, the point was just such a family you could not buy for love nor money, and just such a girl would be just the right thing for her boy Manoj.

As it is with things of speed, speed gathers, and all number of hitherto disparate particles get flung together magnetized by the slipstream, a fast train in motion, its cargo clitter-clattering behind it towards its inevitable destination. The Laws of Physics are older than us, much older, they know what they are doing or certainly purport to, given that they are seemingly unswayable, and we can either fight or surrender, but either way the result is the same.

Q.E.D.

And so it was that Manoj Prabhakar, just so happened to be in Poona on work at the very same time that Mrs. Prabhakar leant forward a little too eagerly, her fat little elbows – if we can call them elbows so buried amongst well fed flesh was the bone – slipping off the armchair, saying to Mrs. Diwan who mentioned Bina's comment about Farida's daughter, 'You know, I am thinking that maybe this girl would be a nice match for my Manoj…I mean naturally we would have to see her and all of that, but I am thinking ki maybe he might like her. You know how he is, doesn't want to settle down, but I am thinking that this girl, such a good family, such an old family, class, not flashy, this sort of girl he would like. Oh my God, you know he is in Poona, right now!' She tried not to look too excited as this latest realization dawned on her. She knew, coming from a shrewd trading family that it is never a good tactic to look too keen. But this was too much. Manoj in Poona at exactly the same moment she hears about this girl! It must be written in the stars. If only my astrologer was still alive!

'Really? He's in Poona now?' said Mrs. Diwan. 'What are the chances! I am sure we could arrange a meeting… but will Manoj go?' adding 'Apparently she is quite lovely.' This was not the first conversation Mrs. Diwan had had with Mrs. Prabhakar about

Manoj's prospects, and she was keen to not to be caught in the same circular conversation for yet another year, hoping that this would be the spawn for the salmon so to speak. Mrs. Prabhakar was not one to hold her worries close to her chest and often Mrs. Diwan found Mrs. Prabhakar's head on her shoulder, her fleshy cheek pressed against her silken sari sleeve, tears, snot and all. 'I just do not understand how a young man of 30 does not want to get married, yah. He simply refuses to meet anyone I suggest,' she would wail.

But now, heartened by this latest promising prospect Manoj's mother seemed cheered and unusually resourceful. 'I am thinking, ki maybe… maybe we don't tell him there's a girl,' she said putting her hand on Mrs. Diwan's as if it was Mrs. Diwan who needed reassurance. 'Maybe we say Bina has some family friends in Poona and would he like to go for dinner, I know he gets sick of hotel food when he is working. He might even be wanting some company by now. Certainly, some good home-made khana. But…how will we approach the family??'

'Bina told me Farida Avari is keen to find a match. I am sure she will agree to an informal meeting. It is the best way with these youngsters, if they know we are plotting they go running, if they think we are not bothered they come galloping!'

And so it was that Manoj Prabhakar, "dropped in" for dinner at The Avari's once stately now crumbling family home on Balthazar Drive, Poona, on the 17th of September 1988 at about or exactly 7.30 pm and that at about or exactly the time that he walked through the gate, at about or exactly that time, a scurrying dust cloud, that this time was not Raju, but was in fact Mehnaz, running late having forgotten that there was a guest coming for dinner, rushed through the gate, straight into him, her breasts pounding full pelt against his turning chest, and the clitter-clatter of the train, as quickly as it had started, stopped.

Its cargo delivered. Squarely deposited.

Q.E.D

The gate clanged. The dust motes settled. All was still. The tempest began.

CHAPTER 4

The jury is out on whether speed is heaven sent or only for nitwits and the naive. Let's examine the historical evidence. *'More Haste Less Speed,'* admonishes one. *'Only Fools Rush In Where Angels Fear To Tread,'* warns another, these perhaps having had their fingers burnt and proceeding to project their disappointment and foreboding on the rest of us. The *Love at First Sight* brigade trot out their artillery, quivers full of cupid arrows, seeming somewhat smug as if they were the more liberated, the more bohemian, the more blessed, as if they'd been to Woodstock and danced with daisy wreaths in their hair, leaving those who had taken let's say a fair few dinner dates or even a few years to discover the irresistibility of their respective spouses, doubting their union and hoping the slow dance doesn't play at the party.

Mehnaz's sensible friend Simran always told her that when you buy a new dress don't rush to wear it when you go home. Leave it in the bag and then try it on in a few days and if you still like it then keep it. This was all well and good for Simran, but Mehnaz was the kind who would try it on in the shop and if she liked it would ask for her old one to be wrapped, and walk out into the street then and there in her new one, not because she was impetuous, or spoilt, but because she just couldn't help herself. Who knows whether it was this immediacy, this un-held back full throttled delight that she brought to everything, whether it was this, or whether it was a fated chemistry, the kind that no one can predict or decipher, the kind that just is, or whether in fact it was the shocking presence of sudden maleness, without preamble or warning, made all the more startling in this all female house, where all arms were smooth, where breasts were breasts not chests, where only the lightest of down could be traced upon upper lips, whatever it was, in that moment of collision at the gate of Balthazar House, *something* happened. Something beyond word or definition, that all who have felt will know and all who haven't will long for, something that took hold of her like an electric storm that was at the same time the magnetic sweep of an ocean, she the limpet on the tide, unstuck, alternately swirling in the heady surf and pulled without protest into the current.

For Manoj's part, colliding with her, into her soft, plump, generous body, shocked him in a different way. All his nerve endings went into a sort of overdrive unable to compute this most bewildering and be-witching of sensations. She was both the most sensual thing as well as the most motherly, like being suckled and fucked all at the same time. Yes, like being a baby and a beast all at once. It felt illicit. He might have mumbled something, she might have stuttered something. Or maybe they just stood there. It's hard to say exactly, the way you can't quite remember a dream, catching at strands and flashes of it as its truth vanishes from view.

Far, far overhead, Kalina flew. Glancing occasionally downwards upon the turning earth far, far below, she caught a flash out of the corner of her eye. A flash that happened when a gate clanged, at about or exactly 7.30 pm, at the entrance to a once stately, now crumbling house on Balthazar Drive. Or perhaps it didn't flash. It glinted. An interesting word. Kalina slowed, her eyes narrowed, but she flew on.

CHAPTER 5

Whatever order had hitherto presided over the dining table, that evening it went to the wind. Farida usually subliminally highly strung, was more obviously so, trying to look relaxed and not succeeding as she busied herself in the dining room, her nerviness exacerbated by Mehnaz, who tonight of all nights was not yet back. Mehnaz was always back by 7pm, certainly no more than about quarter past. Even if bringing one of her college pals back with her to join the family for dinner, they would come through the gate by then, Mehnaz stopping first to bring Ferangiz her evening tea if she was early enough, or going via the verandah to say hello to her aunt if she was later, a habit that irked her mother, irked her more that she would like to admit, made more irksome by the fact that she knew Mehnaz did it without intention, as if it was the most natural thing in the world. Nevertheless, that's how it always was, Mehnaz home by 7 - 7.15.

So when she had casually mentioned to her daughter that a guest would be joining them for dinner she didn't make too much of a point of asking her to be back on time, especially as Bina had phoned her again today on behalf of Mrs. Prabhakar – there had been five phone calls on Mrs. Prabhakar's behalf this week already and one from Mrs Prabhakar directly – to once again ensure that it would be a casual evening, the boy just dropping in after work, please no one to dress up, otherwise he would suspect immediately, and, wouldn't it be better if Mehnaz also did not know about anything, so that if love were to bloom, it could do so as naturally as methi grows in the Punjab, this last bit added by Bina by way of her own poetic license. Farida, who as we know had her own private hopes for the success of this spontaneous rendezvous, duly made very little of it indeed.

Between us, she did ask Hema to make an extra special dinner for this evening, not so fancy as to seem that they were going especially out of their way, but not so every day as to risk not leaving a memorable impression. Knowing that Almaz always asked Hema as soon as she woke up what they were going to have for dinner, Farida was careful not to give Hema her instructions until Almaz had found Shanaz from whichever alcove of the house she was wisping about in that morning, and the two had left for school, Almaz chattering ahead and Shanaz humming absent-mindedly behind. Farida didn't want to raise any unnecessary alarm bells and given that Almaz's food radar was as sensitive as a sophisticated meteorological weather system, this was prudent. The slightest gastronomic isobar shift and she would know immediately that something was up.

Farida had been giving particular thought to what they should have for dinner. Chicken for sure, this went without saying, but she wondered whether the boy would like his chicken with the skin on or off.

She considered calling to check with Mrs. Prabhakar but then thought this might look a little too eager and over-accommodating, and bristling defensively at her own thought, it certainly wasn't as if she was. She was keen for the meeting, if only to start the ball rolling, to get Mehnaz into circulation so to speak, but she didn't want to give the impression that she was keen on this particular boy. That was yet to be seen. Bina seemed to like him and Farida trusted Bina's opinion. 'I've only met him once or twice, at the odd Diwali party,' she said. 'Seemed nice enough. Well turned out, well-spoken, doing very well. I think he's worth a look Farida. His mother is a little, shall we say… talkative. But harmless. Apparently, he's not interested in the family business, wants to do his own thing. That's a good sign.' Yes, that was a good sign, thought Farida. She did not want Mehnaz getting embroiled in a family that were dog toothed into each other so much that you couldn't extricate yourself and have your own life. Or one that would lay such a claim to Mehnaz that once she was in their fold, her own family would become a small satellite constellation, which they would summarily eject out of orbit at the first chance. This boy had his own mind and his own job, and this was a very, very good sign indeed.

She decided on the skinless chicken. Most people preferred it that way. Too bad for Almaz. Ok, so chicken curry, with fried onions and raisins, Hema's special dal, she would get out the good rice, the long grain basmati and some saffron. Was saffron a bit too much? Saffron made everything seem like an occasion. No saffron. Boondi raita for sure, who doesn't love boondi raita. What vegetable? Potatoes? Everyone likes potatoes, but it's a poor man's food she thought, I don't want him to think we are church mice. Something a bit more, I know, we could have baingan. And I'll ask Hema to make some rotis. He will be wanting home-made rotis after all that hotel food, like Bina said. With ghee.

Menu resolved she duly gave instructions to Hema, who grumbled that it was a little late to be told to make the special dal. Farida Madam knew that she liked to soak it longer, now it will not be as good she said, taking her annoyance out on Raju, who she dispatched to get some fresh boondi from the sweet shop down the road and some more onions while he was at it and hurry up no dawdling, she yelled after him as he took it slower than his customary snail's pace. She knew Farida Madam well enough by now to know that this was not an ordinary dinner, having worked for her for more than 30 years. Or was it longer. No one really knew, the way no one can really remember their pubic hairs arriving, no one ever knows that exact moment when the first curly hair breaks through, but then suddenly it seems that they've always been there, as if they've snuck in overnight and built a thatch while no one is looking. Not that we are in anyway comparing Hema to the short and curlies – though now

24

come to think of it, she was rather low to the ground at 4 foot 11, and no amount of coconut oil could tame that curly havoc of hair that she nevertheless persisted in trying to plaster to her head – least of all making any parallels to possible maturity. Hema was known for her temper and wanting to do things her way. There was no trimming her, no keeping her in check, you took Hema as she was, because that's how she came, no one ever questioning it in much the same way as you would not question an ill-tempered temperamental rhino, least of all an ill-tempered temperamental curly haired rhino that made great chapatis and unequalled dal. Besides Hema adored that family as they did her. Neither party may have quite used the term adored, but under the skin of it that's how it was, being as we are most crotchety with the people we love the most. Raju excepted.

In all the years of working for Farida Madam, Hema frowned, as she picked the dal, Madam had never ordered the dinner in such a strange way. She had seemed odd. Was she whispering? Maybe that was it, Madam had sort of whispered the dinner order. It made her nervous. Hema was not really the kind to feel nervous and her goitre started to itch. And, she thought, Madam had asked for the chicken with the skin off. Everyone knew that Almaz liked the skin on. Madam would do anything and everything for her girls, and now she was ordering the wrong chicken.

While Hema frowned over all of this, Farida was in her bedroom, frowning over which sari to wear. Why could we just not tell Mehnaz about all this, she thought suddenly angry, instead I am going to have to wear some sort of semi rag and not give the right impression. What has happened to courtship these days! It is all cloak and dagger and not even an embroidered cloak! In the end she decided to wear a sari that Mehnaz loved, a light green cotton, with white embroidered flowers along the edge, suitably spring like, but not one to attract obvious remark or attention, a sari for beginnings thought Farida and plus as it's Mehnu's favourite that can only be a good omen. She relaxed a little bit at the thought and then jumped out of her skin as the phone rang loudly in the hall. It was again Bina, calling from Delhi. This time not dispatched by Mrs. Prabhakar who by all accounts had so worn herself out with nervous tension and anticipation rolled into one, that she had had to lie down in her bedroom with the curtains drawn and the air-conditioner on, followed later by some laddoos and tea to revive her. 'Good luck, Fari,' Bina said, 'let me know how it all goes. The main thing is be casual, be casual, ok. What have you told the family?'

'Nothing yet! I am practically bursting Bina! You know I cannot keep a single secret! But I know it will be best like this. Otherwise I will also have all manner of objections from everybody, especially Ferangiz. I'm going to say that the son of a family friend of yours is in town and will be dropping in for dinner, he's all on his own here, which is the truth, it has to be the truth whatever I tell Ferangiz even if it's not the full truth, because she will immediately know if not. I was thinking I will tell her after she is back from school and her tuition students have left, just before her tea. I've already told Mehnaz this morning that we have a guest from Delhi tonight, she was in a rush to get to college, so she barely heard, but she's always back by 7pm so…. Shanaz is Shanaz and Almaz is mainly going to have to be managed about the chicken situation.'

'The chicken situation?'

'Nothing, nothing!', said Farida quickly. Why could she not ever keep her mouth shut. 'I'll call you tomorrow morning. Thank you so much for everything Bina, wish me luck, hanh!'.

CHAPTER 6

Despite Bina wishing her exactly that, things did not go well with Ferangiz. Farida had been feeling nervous all afternoon as she knew that coupled with her inability to keep a secret, was Ferangiz's ability to sniff one out in a trice. She just did not want Ferangiz to get a whiff of anything, because she knew exactly what Ferangiz would say. 'You are doing what?', in that way of hers that would have made Julius Caesar, Genghis Khan and their conjoined armies shrivel and hurriedly retreat. 'Mehnaz is 19 years old, Farida, are you out of your mind? What are you even thinking? She has her whole life ahead of her. And besides, Mehnaz is perfectly capable of looking after herself.' Farida bridled at the thought of this imagined exchange, especially that very last bit, the way Ferangiz spoke as if she knew Mehnaz better than anyone else did, as if she could see into her very future, like she knew her niece's every step, as if she had a special claim to her, as if their relationship trumped all others, as if Mehnaz was *hers*. Farida got by turns agitated and angry, as she paced the house that was now empty – bar Hema grumbling to herself in the kitchen – thinking of when would be the right moment, what exactly to say, how to start, how to sound casual, casual like Bina had instructed, until she thought she would just about implode with anxiety. In an attempt to calm herself down she sought familiarity and squeezed herself into the blue and white rattan rocking chair, plucking at the fraying strands – she must get that rethreaded soon – the chair that had been with them longer than even Hema and that each of the children had been rocked in and that all the adults could still just about squeeze into, even if their thighs pushed through the sides, like the tops of bread loaves poking out of a tin. More than the china so neatly displayed in the lounge cabinet, more than the old invaluable books that lined their shelves, more than the last remaining solitaire Farida still wore round her neck, this rocking chair was the true family heirloom. She rocked herself, quite unaware that she was rocking harder and harder and faster and faster as her agitation rose until Hema appeared in the doorway looking at her with frowning concern. 'Madam, everything is ok?'

Farida stopped mid-rock embarrassed to have been caught so clearly at odds with herself and squeezed herself out of the chair and on to the sofa, but not before Hema turned and then returned with some tea, thumping it in front of her in wordless instruction. Farida was by now in such a state that she almost confided in Hema, just about managing to hold it in, feeling angry again that her sister managed to always be so contained in a way that was never within her own capability or grasp as she gulped down the hot, sweet liquid with relief. Maybe it was because papa had died so soon after she was born and only Ferangiz had had the benefit of his forceful, solid presence, instead of being brought up solo by her grieving mother the way she was. Yes, maybe that was it. She felt better, consoled by the possibility that it was not her fault.

In the end, calmed by the tea, she decided on a strategy. She would take her sister the sweets that Raju had mistakenly bought from the sweetshop instead of the boondi that Hema had ordered, she would take the sweets over to her after Hema had served Ferangiz her afternoon tea. Yes, that would give her a reason to make the visit to Ferangiz's verandah.

For a view of the house-plan, lest it not be apparent, Ferangiz had the left wing as you face the house, with two spacious rooms – one her bedroom, the other a large study, both opening onto a sweeping verandah that curved around to the back – taken by her especially so that she could have the quiet and privacy that she liked for her marking and studying and writing, plus it suited her to be away from the rabble, which is privately how she regarded most of the household. This arrangement like so many of the arrangements in the house had come about by default. Farida unable to countenance anything worse than being anywhere but in the thick of it, had her bedroom just off the lounge and dining room, and though smaller she was happiest there never far from earshot or arms' length of anything, whereas to reach Ferangiz's lodgings you had to walk round the outside of the house via the voluminous verandah. Of course, Ferangiz had intentionally made this so, having closed and bolted a few interlocking doors that otherwise would have opened her quarters to the rest of the house.

Now we have the lay of the land.

Yes, thought Farida, that will give me a legitimate reason to visit, and the sweets will give me a perfect way to explain that this young man Manoj is going to be coming for dinner. She resolved to keep an eye on the gate for the last student to leave, which was usually about 5pm unless Ferangiz decided to turn them into her latest improvement project, in which case they would stay a little longer to get that bit more instruction, which unbeknownst to them yet would make all the difference to how far they later got in life.

As someone once said, when we wait we are powerless, and that was never more true than this windless afternoon, while Farida anxiously waited for Ferangiz's students to leave. She heard Hema clanking in the kitchen as she prepared Ferangiz's tea and then watched her carefully carry the tray out to the verandah at 5.25 pm, returning quickly, even Hema not ever daring to linger in Ferangiz Madam's presence. This was the cue for any straggling students to leave and as if by clockwork, she saw the last of them file out quietly by the side-gate.

Now was the time. Farida took the box of sweets from the fridge and then taking a deep breath, looking heavenwards for all the help she could get, she made her way as nonchalantly as she could, which was not very nonchalantly at all, to the verandah.

Ferangiz was sipping her tea, head bent over her books, cup in one hand, red pen in the other.

'I brought you some sweets to have with your tea,' said Farida.

Ferangiz looked up frowning. 'Why have we got sweets? Did someone bring them?'

'No, Hema sent Raju to buy some boondi but he bought sweets by mistake.'

'Something has to be done about those two, between them we will be wiped out of house and home. Why is Hema wanting boondi?'

Farida, despite herself took a deep breath in.

'A family friend of Bina's is dropping in for dinner, she's making boondi raita,' she said as casually as she could.

'Why are you whispering Farida? Who is coming for dinner?'

Speaking up a little bit more but then her nerves over calibrating in the other direction, Farida almost shouted.

'A family friend of Bina's!'

Ferangiz looked up properly this time, her eyebrows arching above her glasses, though it was unclear whether this was in response to Farida's announcement or the decibel in which it was delivered.

'Oh,' she said. Ferangiz did not have much time for Bina, considering her a meddling socialite who only had time for parties, in fact regarding her not much less favourably than how she judged most people from Delhi. 'Who is this friend?'

Farida held her breath. 'Some young man called Manoj.'

Ferangiz's cup halted. 'Young man? Why on earth would a young man want to be coming here for dinner with us?'

'He is the son of Bina's friend a Mrs. Prabhakar, and he is here on work for a few weeks, Bina mentioned to her that we, I mean I live here and said that if Manoj needed some company and home cooking that he should drop by. So he is coming along this evening.'

'I see,' said Ferangiz.

There was a short silence that Farida thought she best use to turn to go, knowing the less she said the better. Just as she reached the far end of the verandah however, Ferangiz said in a quiet voice, 'How strange that we have not until this time had any friends of Bina's drop in from Delhi. Other than the fact that all the girls are too young for any such shenanigans, and even you would not entertain such nonsense, I would almost say you have a hand in this Farida.'

Thankfully before Farida started to incriminate herself by babbling a protest, Ferangiz continued.' What time is this guest coming?'

'About 7.30 I think...'

'Take these,' Ferangiz said holding up the sweet box to Farida unopened, Farida having to scale the verandah again to take them, while Ferangiz returned without a further look at her to her marking.

CHAPTER 7

It was 7.25 pm and Farida dressed casually in her green and white sari, fiddled with the china in the cabinet debating whether to go and sit in the lounge or stay here in the dining room and pretend to be busy. Where on earth was Mehnaz? Where was she? Would nothing ever go her way? Would the stars never align for her, make her life easy even once? The familiar anger rose in her, an anger that if you saw Farida's sweet eager-to-please face you would never know lurked underneath.

'Ma, who did you say was coming for dinner?' shouted Almaz from the phone table in the hall. Her mother didn't answer, so preoccupied was she by the evening's botched arrangements. 'Someone from Delhi yah,' Almaz said filling in her own blanks to whichever buddy she was talking to. 'I hope this doesn't mean we will eat late Ma!' Almaz had a habit of conducting at least two conversations at any one time, either as a means to hold as much attention from as many people as possible or to chatter twice as much, one could never be quite sure.

A moment later, outside, the gate clanged. Farida jerked as if a lightning bolt had gone through her, all the tensions of the day going off like a pair of giant cymbals in her head. It was about or exactly 7.30 pm.

CHAPTER 8

In the sixth sense that we all have with things –
whether we acknowledge, ignore or deny these
inklings – everyone knew that *something* had
happened. Maybe everyone knew that something had
happened in a way that they also knew that nothing
would ever be the same again, but perhaps that is
loading far too much certainty on a timorous feeling
that everyone felt nonetheless. When talking about it
later, much later, after Mehnaz had left, they would
each discuss what they had felt in that moment when
Mehnaz and Manoj walked in together through the
door.

Almaz claimed that she had instantly stopped
talking, which from what we know of Almaz is the
equivalent of saying that a Japanese bullet train went
from 300mph to 0 in 3 seconds, though given the
quality of Japanese engineering this would have
happened smoothly whereas the way Almaz
described it, it was more like her words just fell out
of her mouth, tumbling to the floor, vowels coming
loose on the way, the way a car driven off the edge of
a cliff falls noiselessly into a canyon, pebbles and dust
toppling silently with it into the void. In other words
– if we are to be straight forward about it – Almaz was
dumbstruck. Was this because she was not expecting
to see a strange man in the doorway, least of all a
strange, good-looking man standing next to, actually

quite *close to* her sister or was it because she could sense that thunder had just clapped? Who knows. What she claimed, when they would talk about it later, is that she knew something *big* had happened. She even said she had dropped the phone, leaving her friend dangling from the cord mid chatter, but this may have been a characteristic Almaz embellishment, always seeking as she did to make life more interesting and dramatic than it actually was.

Farida meanwhile was unsure whether to look happy that Mehnaz was back just in time or deliberately nonchalant about Manoj's presence, so thrown was she with the two appearing together in the doorway, that her mouth formed a perfect O that stayed that way before dropping some seconds or minutes later into her more customary sideways D in cheerful and she hoped casual greeting. Her mind mostly too busy with competing worries, fancies and anxieties to notice the true temper of a situation, knew instantly that *something* had happened, something she had not planned for, something that she would have no control over, something that she didn't yet know Ferangiz would hold against her in the most unforgiving of ways, something that would change the tinkle of their home to a tomb.

But…we fly ahead, wait time, wait, stay with us in this moment that everything changed. She did not share anything of this with the others in the later recounting, indeed in the much later days did not like to recount it at all. What she did say is, looking back maybe it was the fact that Mehnaz wasn't saying anything, that Mehnaz seemed not frozen exactly, what was that look on her face…was it shock…Mehnaz, always so easy in her skin, so natural with everybody, so utterly herself always, was not. Shanaz too, in her perpetual dream state, seemed to register them, the absent humming that followed her everywhere in a way that she was completely unaware of but drove everyone else demented – such that living with Shanaz was a bit like living with an absentminded professorial bee – her humming, as she walked through the corridor and saw them in the doorway, momentarily stopped. She momentarily carried on again, but the significance of the hum hiatus cannot be overstated, the last time in living memory this happened being during the earth tremor, when maybe it had not stopped but just been drowned out by the greater hum of the earth.

What happened next was by all accounts a blur. Everyone remembered the initial sighting, but no one, not one of them, fully remembered what happened next. There was perhaps some small talk – Farida taking over to fill the silence. Farida always filled the silence, not being able to abide awkwardness or discomfort of any kind, she could always be relied on to fill it with some soothing question or comment – often if we are to be honest, inane – that filled the spaces in between. 'How nice you could join us, beta,' or 'How long are you here from Delhi, Manoj,' or 'Where are you working in Poona, beta,' or 'Where are you staying while you are here, Manoj,' or some such combination of all or some of those would have filled the silence like icing from a cake nozzle or putty from a plaster gun depending on your point of view. And Manoj, quite unsure how to appear decent, while still feeling quite, quite indecent in the presence of this girl, this woman, this mother-maiden would have broken his silence possibly with relief, released into the familiar murmur of niceties, that would allow him to exhale, disengage from his groin and engage his brain. A co-lawyer had told him once that he had been at a party chatting to this other attractive lawyer and that he had had an erection sitting right there, in full view of everyone, trying to grin and nod and listen to what she was saying, all the time his trousers standing to attention, both of them pretending that they didn't know what was happening and everyone else trying not to look or laugh. Manoj had snorted with laughter when he heard this, you poor dog, he had said, and now here he was in danger of the very same thing. We become what we laugh at, someone had said that once to him too.

He was saved not by the bell, but by the baingan. Dinner was served, and with the dining table as ample cover, Manoj was safe. The family gathered. There was some confusion as to where everyone should sit, and Manoj sensing he was the only man in the house, rather presumptuously in the manner of old Delhi emperors, after a quick scan was about to lower himself into the chair at the head of the table, when Ferangiz joined them for dinner, the way she always did arriving once everyone was present. There was an awkward moment when Farida not wanting to offend her guest did not want to ask him to move to the main flank of the table, but equally did not want things to start on a let's say inauspicious note – though we all know that this would be a tremendous understatement – by him commandeering Ferangiz's chair. Mehnaz just about recovering saved the day, by beckoning him to come and sit next to her, but not before Ferangiz had clocked the boy's arrogant sense of place, no manners, she thought, thinks he's the blooming major-domo.

Ferangiz being Ferangiz, for all her earlier reprimand, was faultlessly polite, her presence so commanding that Manoj quite forgot about his near trouser-tent imbroglio and was hauled into her force field, strong enough to break any spell. Inevitably the centre of gravity coalesced around her, with Ferangiz holding court. They conversed in the way that people who don't know each other well do, with formality and polite interest, sometimes feigned.

'What brings you here, young man?' asked Ferangiz.

'I'm in charge of the legalities on a corporate deal; the firm want me on tap for any potential hitches. So I'm stuc..stationed here for 6 weeks. Staying at The Imperial.'

'Your mother is a friend of Bina's I understand?'

'Yes, socially. In fact, I believe it was Bina Aunty who suggested to her I should drop by, I must say, it's great to have some home cooking after 3 weeks of restaurant food, I'm so sick of it!' he said taking a chapati brought in by Hema who looked at him with suspicion.

'Yes, so Farida told me,' said Ferangiz, 'Bina was here last week, did you meet with her?'

Farida stiffened.

'I've only met Bina Aunty a few times actually,' said Manoj.

Farida's nose pinched as she took an anxious intake of breath, she really did not want this conversation continuing in this potentially precipitous vein, her mind scrambling about unsuccessfully for a suitably casual interjection.

'Oh?' said Ferangiz. 'Somehow I got the impression you were practically family.'

This dangerous trajectory was broken by Almaz's yelp when she saw there was no skin on the chicken. She was silenced by a look from her mother, who was nonetheless grateful to her for the interruption, jumping in with a remark about the food at The Imperial or such like. Averted!

Naturally none of this escaped Ferangiz's attention. While conducting her perfunctory conversation with this, how shall we say, overly confident young man, Ferangiz's radar was all the while picking up the minutest of signals that emitted from Mehnaz, and those that passed – or didn't pass – between the pair. It did not escape her attention, that neither looked even once at the other, studiously so, and that this in itself spoke more than any exchange. Nor did it escape her that that Mehnaz was unusually quiet, actually not merely quiet…*still*… yet not stagnant, still in the way of a pregnant pause, still in the way of stopping to receive something of magnitude, still in the way everything goes quiet before a storm. Although Ferangiz would never contribute to the post-mortems that the rest of the family would indulge in, she knew then with absolute surety as the lead took weight in her stomach, with the sickening surety and certain predictability of an irreversible chemical reaction, that *something* most definitely had happened. Even that they would never be the same again.

So when at the end of the evening Manoj took his leave, and Ferangiz heard Farida say, in the way of an icing nozzle flourishing letters on a cake, 'You must come again next week, beta. Come as many times as you can while you are here in Poona, ok?' Ferangiz wanted for the first time in many, many, many years to scream. She wanted to scream to make something that could not stop, that could not be changed, for it to stop, for it all to change, for the molecules to reverse, to undo their fated bonding and for all that was, to return. She left for her quarters without saying goodnight – though this could have easily been seen as her customary aloof exit – the scream that was rising silently in her throat threatening to engulf her the way it had all those years ago, blocking out all words of polite farewell, the rising panic and latent grief not yet turned to rage, nor yet apparent to the world.

Mehnaz normally sensitive to the slightest emotional tremor was on this occasion distracted by her own personal quake and she did not mark her aunt's abrupt departing. No. She was accompanying Manoj to the gate. This was neither complicit, nor vocalized, nor agreed. It just was. Manoj, left alone with her for the few slow minutes it took to walk to the tall rusting gate, once more felt the stirring, almost instantly and as disturbing. It wasn't as if he was new to women, far from it, so we can't put this down to fettered hormones. Priti back in Delhi, was only one amongst many. And although he spent the most time with her – or more precisely between her legs – it would be fair to say that nothing was further from his mind in this moment, than Priti's athletic manoeuvrings and eager ministerings. They walked side by side to the gate in silence, and when they got there she – still not having said a word – reached up on tiptoe to lift the heavy iron clasp that held the two gates together, in a way that quite unintentionally and therefore even more alluringly exposed the curve of her breast at the same time as the tilt of her mother-maiden rear. In that moment, Manoj did something that even for him was out of character and frankly so forward as to be scandalous. He reached up, reaching for the clasp with her, in a way that could have been construed from a distance to be assisting, but seen up close his body moved right up behind her, more than grazing her, almost pressing, but not quite, and then lifting the clasp with her, hand over her hand, the gate opening a crack, he not moving away, she neither, then holding her wrist bringing her arm down with his and laying it on her flank, still standing behind her, shocking both of them. If the eyes of the house were not upon them, Manoj might have been tempted to pull her in closer, and after that who knows what, but he was no fool. He turned her around, the mother-maiden facing him with neither resistance nor submission – there it was again, that innocent earthiness – 'I'll be back for more chapatis.' he said, his fingers reaching forward and running over her lips, every bit of her hitherto un-touched 19 year old body going up in flame, like an inferno in the wind.

He left.

Mehnaz stood there for some time, not moving, barely standing. She did not know what she was made of anymore, hot molten liquid seemed to have replaced her flesh and warm blood, her heart pumping some sort of honeyed lava through her. She touched her lips with her fingers as if to check, to feel. 'Mehnaz! What are you doing? Come inside!' her mother shouted and she hypnotically obliged. But not before turning once more to the gate, reaching for the clasp, to imagine once more that pressing male weight against her. She latched it and turned back to the house. All molecules changed.

Behind her, a black feather as long as an arm from shoulder to fingertip, floated downwards, see-sawing on the shifting currents yet holding a steady line, down, down, straight down, landing pin point first into the red earth like a quill, before falling gently on its side at the gate of Balthazar House where Raju would find it as he came in the next morning, oblivious of its import, picking it up and because of its extraordinary length and striking plumage, proudly adding it with a flourish to his broom.

Part Two

HOMI

CHAPTER 1

If Kalina's wings were to flap backward through time, a mere few long, languorous beats would take us u-curving into an altogether different age, when the tall gate at Balthazar House was proud and shiny, no hint of rust or the rust to come, and through which society's shiniest people, with medals on their breasts, silver on their arms and proud ambition in their hearts came and went. The yard still laden with fruit trees of every kind and in that sense unchanged, had a different quality, as if the leaves were younger and shinier, less dusty, the mangoes, badams and pomegranates all gleaming like botanical jewels, fresh and glistening and bursting with riches.

To look upon the façade of the house – the tall pillars at the front, standing in a great arc holding up the grand flanks whose sweeping verandahs were practically esplanades, the walls maintained in the whitest of whitewash, the bamboo chiks backed with a deep green cotton keeping the air around the house soft and cool, the stone floors a high polish – to look upon all of this was to look upon a time of grace and prosperity.

It was in this house and in such a time that two little girls grew up, two little girls whose names both began with F, two little girls who as women we have become so far a little acquainted with, two little girls called Ferangiz and Farida, in order of their arrival six years apart into this world. It was in this house at whose helm was a high court judge, a very busy, very important, very imposing man, with an extravagant moustache and an inordinate temper that flared when and only when a moral line was inappropriately crossed, yet was capable of the utmost gentleness especially when it came to the two little girls who ran up to him when he returned through the gates in the evening, calling Dada, Dada! And because as we know, all parents have a favourite even if they claim they don't, there was one little girl who he curled just a fraction tighter in his arms, why hello Izzy he would say, hello my little koel, only he calling Ferangiz Izzy, only he. They would sit together in his study, he and Izzy, while Farida was being put to bed, and they would together run their hands over the bound red leather of the endless Britannicas and Atlases and other volumes of ceaseless wonder and she would pull one out and he would sit in the huge leather armchair and she would clamber on next to him. They would look at the maps of the world, poring over the great mountain ranges, the red and yellow deserts and swirling seas with the red and blue arrows showing the tireless currents, examining closely diagrams of how a sextant worked, drawing together a prototype for a new improved bicycle chain that would allow a woman to ride a bicycle in a sari without it getting entangled. Sometimes they'd sit side by side on the piano, clefs and trebles singing off the keys, he telling her that there were almost a hundred different types of pine needle, and though he never took her to one he told her how that sounded, the soft soundless sound of an old pine forest. Another time she'd listen to the thunder of the maharani of Jhansi's heart or hear about Joan's arc towards triumph or how mercury was unequalled in its inability to be captured. And though he was never the kind of man to break anything intentionally, he one day did snap a defunct thermometer just so he could show her this – but don't touch it he'd say, it's poisonous – and they would carefully chase the little scattering balls of mercurial silver, the judge on his knees on the scarlet rug, both with their cheeks to the ground so they could look at them really close up as they skittled across the shiny floor and he would say to her, never let yourself be captured Izzy, never betray your spirit or your heart, and she would be captivated by this and nod her absolute allegiance. Sometimes they would forgo the study and instead sit on the verandah together as the night drew in and he would point out the birds getting ready noisily for bed, the koels and the mynas, and together they would imitate their song, getting so good that even the birds would turn towards them in confusion. It would have been easy to feel excluded from this tryst and maybe Farida and their mother sometimes did, but it was never done intentionally or with a desire to exclude, plus the engineering of a ball bearing never did exactly capture the other two and neither had the patience to perfect a koel's note so what was to be done.

A quarter beat of a wing takes us forward from this halcyon scene, where all was well, where the day could be predicted and love was guaranteed, to one where two girls aged 12 and 6 look at their mother in dull shock as she tries to find the words to tell them that their father is dead, yes, dead, in a way that tries to let the girls know that they are still safe, that their world has not completely detonated, that she is ever there for them, but failing at this as her voice gives way at first to a whimper and then to a wail. For a brief moment, that felt like a lifetime, the world ceased to turn and when it did, it seemed to turn the other way, going counter to all they knew, the north star plummeting south, nothing any longer what it once was. And where in that very moment without it so being said, it fell upon Ferangiz to take the helm, being the first mate and right hand to her father, despite her legs liquefying, her throat locking, her skin turning to ice in the summer heat, she wilfully sucking all her grief up inside her, a tunnel of howling razor wind, steeling herself just to survive it and hold the family together, for him, for him, all for him.

It was not easy in those days, in a different India, not that it ever is, for a young mother and two young girls to survive, particularly a mother who was prone to panic and flapping where a cool head and a steady heart would have served well. Certainly the situation was not helped by the fact that clearly Judge Bhoman Mistry had not expected to die in a way so sudden and premature that not a single medical encyclopaedia could have predicted it, by going into anaphylactic shock when a poisonous furry caterpillar fell down the inside of the back of his shirt, falling from the old banyan tree that stood outside the high court, falling as he stood talking to his peon, just before he got into the white Ambassador to come home, setting off an allergic reaction that in seconds had stopped his heart, falling dead on to the red earth, his crisp white shirt stampeded by the rising red dust as if a herd of bison had run across him. Gone, gone, gone aged 39, without being able to even gasp goodbye. All that brilliance, all that fortitude, all that honour, a lifetime of protecting and nurturing, gone, gone. Gone. Caught without life insurance to protect and provide for those he left behind. Grief is devastating enough, sudden grief even more so, sudden grief coupled with a thin bank account and the prospect of gritty survival, cruelly tests the endurance of any human heart.

What they did have was the house. Judge Bhoman Mistry had himself inherited the house from his father, the great Chief Justice Firdaus Mistry although for Mrs. Mistry and the two girls this was not quite the gift horse it might seem. They had to manage on a meagre pension increased slightly by the goodwill of the justice service in recognition for Judge Mistry's exemplary though unexpectedly short tenure, which while welcomed with gratitude was hardly enough to keep them in house and home let alone maintain a home like Balthazar. It would be natural at this point to wonder why they did not simply sell the mansion, sell it, move somewhere smaller and use the proceeds to fund the day to day. But to wonder this would be to demonstrate unwittingly an ignorance of the spider's web of land titles in India, where possession is 10/10ths of the law and that the mere hint of a sale would bring innumerable forgotten relatives out of the antique woodwork laying claim to all or part of it, even moving in to ensure it, and setting off lengthy law suits which would need the veracity and intellect of the dear departed Judge Bhoman Mistry to effectively bring to a fair conclusion. The girls' mother who was intimidated even by having to haggle over dinner seating arrangements and to whom conflict was a position best avoided at all costs, avoided all prospect of this and instead decided simply to 'manage'. Besides she knew that were she to decide to sell, the first protest and claim would not in fact come from the lurking relatives but from Ferangiz who had taken to locking herself in the study and immersing herself in Britannica after Britannica night after night. She would never hear of ever selling her beloved father's home.

And so as with all things that are not attended to, either growing worn or wild, the house became both. The whitewash grew less white with time, city soot and grey streaking down the facade in dried tears. The cotton in the chiks too wearing and tearing so that now instead of the singular ocean of cool green light that previously pooled across the shiny floor, now chinks of hot white sun entered, thin flash-beams that interrogated the inside, occasionally catching one of them in the eye causing them to blink like fugitives. The gate started to slowly bubble, the first signs of an irreversible oxidation that would proceed to turn the metal from its smart shiny official green into a muddied, bloodied version of the former. The orchard slowly overgrew, the beds and borders no longer tended in quite the way they used to be, so that creepers took hold and both a weedy green and a red dust settled over the house in a way that none of them despite all their best efforts could ever seem to ever lift. Not at least until much, much later with the arrival of a baby girl who would bring fresh sparkle to their home, but that is another tale, one that we have already heard a little of and will return to in due course. For now, here we remain in the aftermath of Judge Bhoman's tragic death.

In a rare moment of independent decisiveness, the girls' mother decided to completely close up the upper storey of the house. She couldn't bear to sleep in the bedroom up there without Bhoman, Ferangiz never left the downstairs study anyway and Farida trailed behind her mother vicariously hanging on to her tail of anxiety never more than a few feet behind her or far from her side. No, there was no need for the upstairs. She could rehouse the girls' bedrooms downstairs along with her own, plus, she reasoned practically, it would save on cleaning and electricity and they needed to conserve on all that they could. She decided not to move the bed downstairs, for to see the ebony carved bedposts and the wide unoccupied expanse of white sheets was to remind her of her Bhoman in a way that made her heart tighten and choke. So with the help of Bhoman's loyal peon and a couple of extra hands he brought with him from the court, the girls' beds were moved downstairs, along with a few possessions, the wardrobes, the rattan rocking chair, a few lamps – not all of them, as a measure to avoid high electric consumption – and the potted plants. She emptied one of the smaller down-stairs reception rooms of its possessions, stacking some of the more expensive rugs for later sale – just one of those would keep them in school uniforms, food and fees for at least a year – moving the crockery into the dining room cabinet and installing a new single bed and the salvage from upstairs. Farida wanted to sleep in the same bedroom as her mother, so her little bed was put right next to hers, it taking a little bit of negotiation for each to reach their respective mattresses every night, but the scrambling and climbing gave them both incidental comfort as they clambered over each other to get there. Ferangiz insisted on having her bed in the study, no amount of argument would dissuade her, her mother finally capitulating and Ferangiz's bed getting set up on the scarlet rug in the room's centre like a grim mausoleum, a permanent obituary to her father, she lying on it like a sacrificed lamb.

Within all this austere rearrangement, let us not for a moment give the impression that Bhoman's departure meant the departure of society for the family. He was a lauded figure, beloved by many, whose lives he had saved, improved or fought for, his unshakeable moral compass never quivering over what was right and just, no, his gavel was firm and sure, establishing yes this property is rightfully yours, no you have no claim over this land, no you have no right to marry your brother's widow if she doesn't want to what do you think this is the dark ages, yes you do have the right Mrs. Kumar to run the family business, no Mr. Pillai you cannot leave your wife without fully providing for her, not to mention the corporations who had settled their disputes to the tune of crores in his court. Justice Bhoman Mistry was nothing if not principled, nothing if not fair and the goodwill he left in his wake was more than considerable. Therefore many took it upon themselves to make sure that Mrs. Bhoman Mistry who everyone called Chinni, meaning sugar, because she was so sweet, so unimposing, never ruffling any feathers, merging with any situation the way sugar does with tea, was still invited, her presence insisted upon at all the parties and the raffles and the teas as were her daughters', even though Ferangiz had little interest in such affairs but was dragged along, you can't spend your whole life in that study Ferangiz, so much so that Chinni had to consider selling a rug or two just to make sure they could still dress appropriately for the occasions.

It was at one such occasion, the girls now more grown up, many years having passed and time having been ministering its healing – Ferangiz now 19 and grown tall and willowy, having finally moved out of the study into the room near the verandah, Farida only 13 and still in short dresses with sashes, also now in her own room – it was at one such occasion that Ferangiz first met Homi. Well, if we are to be technical about it, they did not actually meet but they were in the same room together.

People say that men don't remember what women wear, they just don't have the same sort of memory or even notice such things the way that women, or certain women, do. But when Homi set eyes on Ferangiz for the first time, it was not actually Ferangiz, it was the hem of her sari, her light blue sari, that he saw first. Even more accurately what he saw first were Ferangiz's long pale feet, peeking out just beneath the sari border, her toenails unpainted, a silver toe ring clasping her little toe, white sandal straps holding them all together, snug but not tight. She was standing in the doorway, poised as if ready to leave, looking outwards in the direction of the front door, so from the adjacent room in which Homi was standing all he could see were the long feet, the grazing hem of the sari, and, something in the stance – a pride and independence as well as a certain impatience – that told him that these feet did not belong to any ordinary girl.

Homi leaned forward, trying not to be obvious about it, so that he could peer around the corner and see who was attached to the renegade feet – what he saw had him halt, in an entirely different way that he did in the army. Maybe the more accurate word is bolt. Bolt. Upright. And through him. A tall girl, as proportionately long and slender as her feet, long lightish brown hair loosely single plaited down to just above her waist, sari wrapped easily around her, a fine nose almost Roman in profile, her mouth intelligent, not gaping nor smiling, and most disconcerting of all – her eyes. He didn't actually get to look into them, being as she was looking the other way, but it was this angle that allowed him to see them without her knowing, beholding the most unusual light grey, kind of steely but with a terrible hidden tenderness, that made his stomach tighten in a way he had never felt, in a way that arose in him a longing and a wonder and a fear. He tilted a little too far forward and he lurched a bit at exactly the same time as her heels turned in full and she walked away from him – away from him! – towards the door, having a quick word with a small, plump lady who judging by their perfunctory familiarity must be her mother, before politely taking leave of Mrs. Chenoy while gesturing at her watch, Mrs. Chenoy nodding understandingly giving her a kiss on the cheek and then she heading out on her loping feet into the setting evening.

Homi panicked, he couldn't let her just vanish! Should he give chase? Follow her out? He stood indecisive and frozen. This was a very un-Homi like thing to do. In fact, though he did not yet know it, it marked the beginning of a time when he would do many, many things that were un-Homi like and over which he would discover he would have no discernible control. The second of these was that he too left the party early. Homi was nothing if not extremely well-mannered, with the kind of charm that you no longer find these days, the kind who was gentle without being limp, gracious without being fawning, courteous without being stiff, softly spoken in an easy, ungrasping way that nevertheless had authority or maybe had authority because of it. One could even go as far as to call him a gentleman in the truest sense of the term, though this might imply a kind of affectation which if you scanned Homi under a microscope inside to out, outside to in, upside down or right way up you'd be hard pressed to find. No, it was simply that now that the girl had left, the whole place seemed empty, plain, so utterly still, like the music had gone even though she had not said much to anyone, and the left over tinkling conversation of the guests sounded to him more like the clearing up of dishes after a party was over, because for him the party was over.

'Going so soon Homi?' said Mrs. Chenoy

'Thank you, aunty, yes I have to get back.'

'It's so lovely to see you, beta, looking so handsome too,' she said, trying not to look too disappointed that Homi though gracious to the utmost had taken no obvious interest in her daughter. 'When will you be home again?'

'I have another day here in Poona then I leave for Lucknow. I've just been posted to the cantonment there for a year. But I'll be back to see Ma and Ruky soon.'

Homi desperately wanted to ask about the girl, but he knew enough about aunties and society – even though he had no appreciable interest in either – to know that to do as much would set off an unwanted reaction of excited tongues, plus Homi being the gentleman he was and an astute one at that knew exactly what Mrs. Chenoy had meant when she'd brought her over-dressed daughter over to meet him saying 'Homi beta, this is Binaiza,' and he certainly did not want to rub salt into that failed match-making wound. So, in a hattrick of un-Homi like happenings that evening, he left the scene without the information he wanted.

CHAPTER 2

Arriving in Lucknow, Homi was distracted. Normally centred, focused, collected, he was edgy. The men noticed it, though they did not say as much – it was not the sort of thing you could say to an officer, even a beloved one. Homi always altogether present, was now not altogether there or rather put more accurately did not *want* to be there – this being the fourth of un-Homi like behaviours should we want to keep count. Why, he berated his fate, did he now of *all* times have to be posted to Lucknow of all places, ten million miles away from Poona?

Homi had not risen quickly in the ranks for nothing, his chess-playing habit from early childhood making him an unusual strategist and coupled with his aforementioned charm and quiet authority, he became at 26 years old, the youngest Lieutenant this regiment or any others had seen in a long while, some saying he was marked for greatness, others saying he had it in his blood, his father and his father before him having both led in the great wars, still others saying unkindly that, that was why he'd had a meteoric rise, which was untrue as Homi had personally earned every stripe and medal. It was this very chess playing mind that knew an unaccompanied Queen or in this case an unaccompanied grey eyed beauty would not be left unclaimed for very long. It made him nervous.

'Arre, Homi what's up,' Lieutenant Balwinder the untameable Sikh that everyone called Billy and who was Homi's best friend would say. 'Ever since we got to Lucknow you have been off mood. Come on yaar, it's not so bad here, snap out of it.' Homi felt foolish to admit that he had been floored by a girl he had not even met, let alone spoken to, so floored that he had not even much noticed Lucknow other than the inconvenient fact that it was miles away from Poona, and that for the first time in his military career he didn't really give a rat's ass for the brigade, wanting to do one thing and one thing only which was to go back to Poona and find the girl.

He shrugged. 'Chalo Billy, let's go for a ride.'

Home for Homi was his horse, Alaska. This is where he went on good days and bad days and in-between days because to ride and especially to ride Alaska was to reset himself. In fact the only request he had made when he was transferred, was that his own horse be transported to Lucknow, which some might say bent the rules, but on this one thing Homi would fervently argue there was no reason why his Alaska could not come with him, saying he made a better lieutenant with his own horse – which if you saw Homi ride her would make a hard case to argue against. Let's skip the details on the wrangling it took to get her here, but in the end Alaska came. The two men walked down to the stables, Homi's head bending towards her 'Hello my Wild Alaska,' in his soft burr and Alaska nickering softly, the syce saddling up for them and then he was on her, her neck twitching, readying, Billy mounting his mare and they were off. On Alaska, Homi could forget about Grey Eyes or at least imagine he was galloping towards Poona, across the plains towards her and he would alternate between the two, switching to oblivion when the pleasure and longing of the latter got too much and then switching back again, Alaska picking up on it and running, running like the wind. When they panted back into the stables, the heavy thought dismounting again with him – 63 more days until Official Leave. 63! He mentally warded off any rooks or fly-by-knights that might be circling the girl right now, virtually sending Alaska's gleaming black body hurtling into their midst, her flying hooves flinging them off the board one by one.

In fact back in Poona, Ferangiz was not surrounded by knights and rooks at least none that posed any threat, partly because she existed in her own world of books and more books and partly because if she was going to look up and take notice then she would do so only for kings. There admittedly many who looked at her wanting to approach but were too afraid to, the chancing pawns who occasionally did, dispatched quickly with one of her blighting looks or more humiliatingly still, not registered by her at all. Nor did she have any idea that many miles away in the north in the ancient city of Lucknow – a place known for its poetry and Urdu and ghazals, actually for *love* – was a young lieutenant called Homi who knew of her existence though she did not know of his yet, and who at this very moment was riding a horse called Alaska, wishing more than anything that he was thundering towards her.

Sixty-three, became sixty-two, became sixty-one, became forty-nine, became thirty-seven, became twenty-seven, became sixteen, became six, five, four, three, two, one. Official leave! Homi boarded the Charbagh train bound for Delhi and thence the express to Poona never more impatient, wondering why despite all the progress and the industrial revolution, trains *still* did not seem to go any faster, in fact seeming slower if that was even possible. Every previously enjoyed stop where Homi would once happily step off, jumping on to the platform to grab a hot samosa or a sweet tea from the station hawker boys, hopping back on the moving train as it started to chug out of the station, each of these previously enjoyed and even awaited interruptions were another delay, another threat, between him and his queen.

He had not yet worked out his battle plan, still unsure how he was going to meet with her, being as he did not even know who she *was* except that she had been at Mrs. Chenoy's party and he still did not want to ask Mrs. Chenoy or anyone else who had been there. He could ask his mother in Bombay – his mother had a knack of seemingly knowing everyone – but this posed the same threat and there was something in him that wanted to find her unaided by his claiming alone. He didn't want the aunties and mothers to sully his gallop across the plains towards her – let's face it in which true legends of love do aunties and mothers make the arrangements – something in him subliminally knowing that what was about to happen would be legendary, or legendary in his world anyway. His sister might know. Ruky, he could ask Ruky. No. She might tell his mother. Maybe as a last resort. He tried to think of the sort of things this girl might do. Library, cinema, swimming, college. College! Maybe he could find her at her college!

He had seven days.

CHAPTER 3

Homi decided to make an entrance. This, just for the record, was un-Homi like too. For all his authority, Homi was a man who liked to lead from the rear. A large part of the reason he had flown up the military ranks was because his men would do anything for him and a large part of the reason for that was because he was like the engine that sits inside a sports car. He was not a showman, he liked to get his hands dirty, he did not particularly care about looking good or sounding good, but he did know how to take people with him. So what Homi did next was about as far away from Homi as it was possible to get. But with only six and a half days to go and knowing he would not be able to be back in Poona for another 70 days, he was taking no chances.

What he did was this. He took a military horse from the Poona cantonment – not Alaska as Alaska was in Lucknow – and he rode to the main girls' college cantering up to it at 3.15 pm when he knew the college day finished. Now to fully picture this scene we have to imagine a few things. First – that the military and civilian parts of the city are broadly separate as they are in most Indian cities. The military part largely untouched for centuries, leafy and sprawling and well maintained, with row upon row of pristine whitewashed buildings complete with its own school, its own hospital, its own ration stores, built so much so that if you didn't want to leave the military cantonment you would never actually need to. And what this meant – certainly then, in those days – was that staff and their families rarely did. So leaving the cantonment and crossing over into civilian territory on horseback was an act that would be remarked upon at the very least as unusual and more likely as downright startling. Secondly, on civilian streets that were as jostling and chaotic as the army cantonment was ordered and quiet it was relatively common to be pushed up against the leathery sides of a holy cow –

or if you were unfortunate against its less than sanitary backside – but not very common at all to rub up against the flank of a horse, let alone a liveried military one. So here too Homi would not exactly go unnoticed. He didn't wear his army uniform…he was tempted though and had he done so this would have been un-Homi activity no.6, let's keep a firm hold on this inventory. But he was not on official duty and therefore it would not be appropriate no matter how appealing the idea. Instead, he wore a white shirt, khaki trousers and riding boots, his horse a large, speckled bay, choosing a friendlier colour than his black Alaska as he did not want to be mistaken for a police charger or for Zorro.

However, regardless of how he tried to soften impressions with his civilian attire and horse's hue, this would not in fact even make a dent into the impression he would make, a young handsome man on horseback, cantering up to the college gates with intent. Jane Austen could not have made it up. Dusty roads, madding crowd, a king of a kind on horseback in search of a girl. It's hard not to swoon. And every single girl coming out of those college gates, swoon they did. His eyes scanned the heads, knowing he'd be able to pick her out from a mile away. This may give the impression that he was calm, in control. In reality, his heart bucked inside him like Alaska on a bad day, hooves in stomach, lurching like a camel. What would he say, how would he say it, he could not even countenance her not being here, she *had* to be here, there was only one decent college in this town, she *had* to be.

Many years of training in the military had taught him a particular kind of surveillance, one that was easy in theory but difficult in practice. It was the art of being completely relaxed and completely alert at the same time, kind of like taking in the breadth of an ocean with the precision of a hawk. It was a way of absorbing the whole scene while being alive to the tiniest shift in detail. Despite the bucking in his chest his eyes were accustomed to doing this unbidden and he caught out of the corner of his eye in the very periphery of his vision beyond the sea of chattering girls under a tree near the college building, a bowed head of light hair in a single plait unchaining a bicycle, unthreading it and slipping the chain round the central mast, slipping her satchel over her head so that the strap crossed her like a sash and mounting easily despite her sari – was that some sort of special mud guard she had – turning to wave at some girls on the college steps who waved back before pedalling towards the gate. Towards him!

Homi was stationed a little distance from the gate also under a tree, not that this in anyway camouflaged him, but it cooled the horse off and he didn't need to be any hotter under the collar than he already was either. There was a single road leading out of the college, so she would have to pass by him, that at least was one condition that simplified rather than complicated matters. But how to approach, which was the moment, how exactly to do this, Homi knew better than to rehearse such moves, knowing that life is unpredictable and that the enemy or in this case the prize would never do exactly as one expects. Therefore, it is simply better once all the ducks have been lined up to respond to what occurs.

He did not want it to look like an ambush which it was very nearly in danger of seeming like, so rather than leap out from under the shade of the tree, a slight pressure of his knees had the bay moving towards the girl as she began to cycle unwittingly towards him. In a Western movie or a bygone time this scene might have seemed normal, like a Highway Man and a Lady in a Carriage, but given this was Poona on a hot afternoon, with rather a lot of girls looking on, him on an off duty horse and she on a bicycle the absurdity of his act suddenly struck him and whether it was nerves or true belly up mirth Homi would never really know, but he would be ever grateful for suddenly breaking into the most irrepressible grin, very almost a chortle, at the very moment that Ferangiz saw him, the man on a horse up ahead, beaming from ear to ear. Now if you had ever had the good fortune to be graced by coming head-to-head with Homi Indrani, especially Homi Indrani bearing a mirthful grin, you would know that it was impossible not to grin back. And that is exactly what Ferangiz found herself doing, grinning up from her bicycle, at a stranger on a horse on a hot Poona afternoon, at about or exactly 3.30 pm.

We already know that Homi is a gentleman. It will not surprise us then that in a trice he was off his horse, so that she would not be forced to look up at him, landing rather showily – he hadn't intended to show off but it did look rather impressive – on his feet as she came alongside on her bike, stepping towards her still smiling though a little less irrepressibly and slightly more nervously this time.

Does this count as the first time? Is the first time when two people lay eyes on each other, or was the first time when he laid eyes on her at Mrs. Chenoy's party 71 days ago? Let's argue about that later. For now, whether it was instinct or whether it was just the way Homi was or whether it was that he knew that this sort of girl would not be swayed by small talk – not that he knew how to do that anyway – or that he knew he only had six and a half days, whatever it was, Homi went straight to it in a way that impressed even himself when he thought about it afterwards. Men could learn a thing or two when it comes to declaring their hearts' desire to women, and this is what Ferangiz heard him say, 'I saw you at Mrs. Chenoy's party 71 days ago, but you'd left before I could say hello. I hoped I might find you here.'

The grey eyes rested on him, a little shocked, a little startled. A little pleased?   The bay harrumphed gently. 'This is Shabash,' he said patting the horse's neck and then stretching out a hand, 'I'm Homi.' He electrified by the feel of hers as she met his, 'I'm Ferangiz'.

'Ferangiz,' he said rolling over the word as if it were something precious.

'I would have come sooner. But I'm posted in Lucknow, this has been my first leave.' As if she'd been waiting, forgetting only he had.

'You're in service?' she said

'Yes. Army. I'm here for six more days.'

Ferangiz reached her hand a little nervously towards Shabash.

'I love animals' she said.

'Can you ride?'

'No. Only my bike.'

'I notice you have a special mudguard.'

She looked at him a little longer before answering this time, he not quite able to decipher her expression. 'Yes, my father and I designed it together, it stops my sari getting caught.'

She smiled.

'That's clever,' he said, the engineer in him looking at it with genuine interest, then looking back at her 'I'll teach you.'

'You'll teach me?'

'To ride. I'll teach you how to ride.'

And that was how it began.

CHAPTER 4

Homi came to collect her from college – this time on his motorcycle – every day for the next six days. Ferangiz changed into her slacks after class and they would go off to the military stables, just for an hour, so that Ferangiz's mother did not get immediately querulous, and Homi would teach her how to ride. She learned so fast, he thought. She had *feel*. Every day the hour stretched a little further, the two drawn together in a way that it was hard to separate and part. With absolute respect but with inescapably erotic awareness – that they both felt – he would adjust her on her horse. Moving her heel down, the heel on the end of that lovely long foot, adjusting her knees, up a bit, tilting her wondrous back, adjusting her sloping shoulders.

Once she was moving more easily, he took her up a notch. 'Let go,' he'd say, 'let go. Let go, Izzy.' She swung to look at him, staring in shock when he called her that – Izzy! No one had called her that since her father! 'You alright, Izzy?' he said. And the way he said it like it was the most natural thing in the world without any awareness of what he'd just done, dialled a hot line right into a long untouched part of her, to a part that felt like safety and rightness and home. And even more than that, if she was to be honest, it thrilled her. It thrilled her young heart and body to hear this handsome man call her that. She nodded. Yes. Yes, she was alright. More alright in fact than she had been in a very long time. And in his presence the long deep fissure that had formed inside her the day her father had died, the long deep fissure that had torn her guts open, the long deep fissure against which she had had to steel herself with a brittle encasement lest she come completely apart, the long deep fissure started to fill. Not to fuse, it never would, nor could, but it filled with a soft golden liquid that some people call love and that Izzy didn't call anything, but she felt it fill her, fill her, so much so that it spilled over the top of the crack and into the rest of her and Izzy, sweet, brave Izzy's heart swelled once more.

It did not escape her mother's notice, her mother who saw that her daughter was returning home flushed, not just with the sun, a flush that one woman can recognize on the face of another, a flush that she too had once felt when Bhoman had courted her. She saw that and recognized it, feeling keenly both Bhoman's absence and maternal vigilance. And before she'd had a chance to fully import that her daughter might have a suitor, a suitor that her daughter actually liked, she spotted something, wait, was that *mud* on Ferangiz's elbow! This practically gave Chinni a heart attack. Was her daughter rolling about in the hay?! She felt herself panic. It was unthinkable in these times to even go about unchaperoned and here there was mud on her daughter's elbow! And to top it all she knew nothing of this boy but that there was a boy she had no doubt.

'Why are you coming back so late from college, Ferangiz?' Her voice was shrill despite trying to keep it even – she knew that to engage Ferangiz you had to keep calm – contributed to no doubt by the fact that she also knew that ultimately, she had no control over this girl. Only one person did, and he was dead and gone. 'Ma, I am learning how to ride,' Ferangiz said, smiling, so bright and happy and as if it were the most natural thing in the world. 'Ride? Ride what?' shrieked her mother.

'A horse.'

One thing it is important to know about Ferangiz was that Ferangiz never lied. Not even a white lie. She was her father's daughter, and in that sense utterly fearless and to her to lie was one of the most ignoble things one could do, not liking to be lied to either. Even if it got her into trouble Ferangiz would take it, she was not going to betray herself for anyone – the blunt truth out.

'A horse? What horse? What kind of horse? Whose horse?!!' her mother was now practically convulsing having expected Ferangiz to perhaps admit that maybe she had met a boy she liked and now this girl was saying she was trotting about on a horse! Bhoman would be spinning in his grave.

'A man called Homi's horse, Ma. He was at Mrs. Chenoy's party. He's teaching me how to ride at the military cantonment.'

Those three little words 'Mrs. Chenoy's party' had the effect that Ferangiz knew they would of calming her mother down. Mrs. Chenoy was not known to have just any riffraff at her parties, quite the contrary in fact, with the guest list including Air Chief Marshalls, Chief Justice's, Chief Justice's wives and daughters, Chief Executives and just about any other kind of Chief you could think of, Mrs. Chenoy having particular pride in knowing so many of society's chieftains and on a first name basis too. Chinni started to breathe again.

'You'll like him, Ma. He's a gentleman. Like Dada.' Ferangiz so happy, smiling at her mother.

Chinni's breath rose with slight excitement this time, maybe this was a genuine prospect for her daughter – a small miracle as she knew that Ferangiz was not easy to please – plus a genuine prospect of the Chenoy calibre was not to be sniffed at, and in the army too. She became a little more conciliatory though still with some residual huffiness.

'Are you going to bring this boy home or just gallivant in the stables, Ferangiz? Have you any idea what people will say!' She knew as soon as she said this that it was the wrong thing to have said, Ferangiz regarding tittle tattle with utmost scorn. It broke the moment of happy communication from her daughter, and she saw the familiar shutters come down in front of her grey eyes, Chinni being locked out again, knowing she had disappointed her daughter, had not met her the way she liked to be met just as so many times before.

'He leaves for Lucknow in two days. So that will be the end of my riding lessons, at least for now.' Ferangiz said, smile gone, turning to leave the room. And that, for now, was that.

CHAPTER 5

On day five, she mounted the grey gelding, breaking into her first gallop a little ahead, grinning proudly back at Homi and he grinning back looking at her – grey eyes, upon that grey horse, hair flying – he didn't think he had ever seen anything so beautiful in all his life. He could cheerfully detonate Lucknow if Lucknow meant leaving her behind.

They rode side by side that afternoon, hearts soaring, hooves flying…he looking over occasionally at her, she glancing occasionally at him. If Ferangiz could be any more perfect than she already was, seeing her fly in that saddle like she'd been born in it cherried the cake, this girl who could ride abreast with him, fearless and free. Of all the afternoons the two would remember, that was the afternoon they would remember the most: warm sun, wet backs, damp hair, a glance, a grin, their lives ahead of them, a sweet knowing in each of their young hearts.

Coming back into the stables a couple of hours later, their horses clopped peaceably alongside each other, 'Mama is wondering why I am coming back so late,' she said dismounting.

'Let me come and meet her,' he said, not skipping a beat.

She halted, looking at him. Their eyes held.

Then Homi leaving his horse came up alongside her, threading the reins out of her hands, turning her shoulders gently towards him, taking her hands in his, the reins still in them. There they stood together next to her horse, he pulling her gently closer, and into that animal silence in the military stable Homi said, 'Marry me, Izzy.'

It was as simple as that.

Love isn't complicated. Don't believe it when anyone says that. It's us, that complicate it. Love, love is simple.

'Marry me, Izzy.'

'Yes,' she said.

There. As simple as that.

CHAPTER 6

Ferangiz's mother was over the moon, over the Sahyadri hills, over the Ghats, over the double rainbow, and over anything else high enough that we can imagine. When Ferangiz said she was bringing Homi to meet her, she had not known quite what to expect, but when this young man, with his kind eyes walked through the gates at Balthazar Drive she knew at once that her daughter had chosen well. He came in uniform, not especially to impress her but as a sign of respect and occasion. She came bubbling out to meet him despite Ferangiz asking her to rein herself in, Chinni was Chinni, what could you do, she came bubbling on to the verandah to meet him, getting bubblier by the second as he approached and she could see that this slim man in uniform, with his steady, twinkling eyes – not to mention the many medals decorating his chest – was just the sort of man she would have dreamt of for her daughter. Farida who was also under strict orders from Ferangiz to behave and not stare, was roped around a pillar, staring out at him, looking rather love-struck herself, as he smiled at her first and treating her like a grown up not a 13-year-old said, 'You must be Farida.'

No prizes then, for originality, as he held his hands out to her mother, taking them both in his, speaking those words that many a man over many an age have said to many a mother or a father, or both if they are lucky enough to still be alive together or respectful of a woman's say. But Homi was not interested in originality, he wanted to say what he wanted to say, so he simply said those words that have been said many a time before, 'Mrs.Mistry, I would like the hand of your daughter in marriage.'

Chinni bubbled and cried and nodded, all regality dissolved in the relief that her eldest had found this fine lieutenant. And if Bhoman could have been there, like Chinni still daily wished he was, he would have smiled his approval at this young man, he thanking her and promising to be a true mate for her daughter.

Though Homi was a man of action, he was a patient man of action prepared to play the long game in war. In love however he was discovering he was impatient. He wanted Izzy to be his *now*, not a long engagement as was customary then, he was impatient for her, the 70 days separation that would be on them tomorrow felt unbearable. He could not do it twice.

'Ma'am, if it so pleases you,' he said, 'I would like to marry Izzy in 71 days' time. Tomorrow I leave for Lucknow and I would like for us to be married the day I return. The 27th of January. I'll take care of all the arrangements.' He said this softly, not pushy, but with a manner that conveyed he was also not exactly requesting permission, even though he somehow made it sound like he was, glancing over at Izzy as he said this, who was flushed with a kind of pride, while Farida swooned.

Love is simple. Love is direct. Love is urgent. Everything else is white noise.

CHAPTER 7

Every day they wrote each other. My dear sweet wild Izzy, he would begin. She loved this, that he saw in her a current of the unpredictable, a longing for wilderness and abandon and tenderness all at once, for what is it we most long for if not to be seen for all we are. *My dear sweet wild Izzy, I am trying to fathom how the hours when I am with you vanish and here in Lucknow every day is interminable. I find myself angry with the brigade for taking me away from you and at the same time rejoicing that next time you will be here with me.*

My dear sweet wild Izzy, he would write, *I wonder what has happened in my life till now, it seems it's only just begun now I have met you. Everything I have been and done now seems nothing, a dream. You are my waking Izzy, you are my waking.* And his fingers would fill with longing as he wrote to her, his heart reaching over the wide plains, the ravines and ranges, over the forgotten villages and the dirty towns, over the millions of lives that one day in India would cross a billion, over towards her, reaching her in her waking and in her sleep.

In others, he would speak of his family. His mother in Bombay, his sister Rukshana in Poona, his father now departed from whom he had learned so much, this another bond that twined them, not that they needed any further twining. Would she go and visit his mother in Bombay? He wished he could take her, but it was right that she should meet his mother before the wedding.

'She will love you Izzy and you will like her very much, of this I am sure. Ruky has told her all about you too, in fact Izzy why don't you and Ruky both go and meet Ma together? That way I feel at least you are being escorted by someone in my family, even if I can't be there.'

Bombay was a short drive to Poona, Poona the young niece, the baby of the family, a kind of familial bond between the two cities that everyone knew of, but no one could quite define. They were to marry in Bombay, this too an untraditional move, the wedding normally falling to the bride's family, home and pocket, but Homi thought it was a ridiculous custom. On the few telephone conversations the couple had, Homi using his scant salary on the ludicrously expensive 'trunk' calls, they would quickly discuss their wedding because despite neither of them caring for ceremony, there had to be a ceremony and neither wanted to break their mothers' and sisters' hearts by denying them that. 'Let's keep it simple, Homi,' Ferangiz said, 'close friends and family maybe 70 people no more,' – by Indian standards a tiny wedding. 'Yes,' he said, 'and then Izzy my love, we'll take the horses and we'll honeymoon on their backs up in Coonoor, we'll ride in pine forests and we'll light wood fires and swim in the lakes and sleep in bungalows.' And the adventurer in Izzy's veins caught flame along with her heart and she wondered what she had done so right to deserve this.

He pored over the letters he received from her, just as she pored over his, his eyes examining every word of her loping hand, loping in much the same way as her walk, so much so that by reading her hand he could almost imagine her walking on the page, long pale foot after long pale foot, plait swinging. 'Nothing makes my day more than seeing your letter in the pigeonhole when I get back to the mess, I see it and I want to throw out my meal so I can get back to my quarters and close the door and be alone with you, my Izzy.'

At other times he would venture towards writing to her his longing for her limbs, though he hesitated, not wanting her to consider him crude or disrespectful but at the same time wanting her to know how much he desired her. He thought he would go demented at the thought of her long white limbs, her skin that flushed and dampened in the heat of the ride, longing for that dampening to be against him, and for her sweat, yes her sweat, not her perspiration, her sweat to mingle with his. He dared to let his imagination unclothe her, though he did not mention this when he wrote, sensing that it might be a step too far. He would imagine himself undressing her, finding himself thinking not about her in her sari but in her slacks, her plain tan nylon slacks that she wore when they went riding, her white shirt catching her breasts as she rose and fell, rose and fell, prompting within him a blasphemous desire to see her rise and fall, rise and fall atop him, and then his mind flashing her naked, completely naked as she did, he rewinding the picture slowly, delaying the pleasure of the culmination, rewinding back to the stables and to her dismounting her horse, long hair falling forward, then back, breasts tipping into her shirt, rear rising, the little flash as she dismounted of the unspeakable jewel that lay between her legs. Oh god. He slowed it down in his head, she coming off the horse, he bending forward to kiss her neck, her long white neck, slowing it down slowing it down, to her mouth, his mouth finding hers, so soft, so firm and then pulling back so he could look at her, her hair dishevelled, so unbelievably beautiful, his hands finding their way to her shirt buttons, oh god, unbuttoning them, and his imagination finding her soft white sloping breasts for the first time, Izzy murmuring, letting him, wanting him, his pulse starting to throb more wildly still, as he, god, could he do this even here in his dreams, would she be upset, sweet 19 year old Izzy, him finding the tops of her trousers, unzipping them, slipping them down along with her

84

knickers, and on the way down as his hands rounded her heavenly bottom, making their way round to the divided white mound between her legs, tentative, is this too far, and his fingers finding their way into the velvet, the two trembling in shock, she finding his trouser buttons, fumbling them open and he finding his way into her, gently, gently so she didn't hurt, laying her down while still inside, and they starting to peak, too quickly both of them and it was over.

Homi was ashamed, he wiped the copious ejaculation off himself, forbade himself any more such thoughts and told himself to concentrate on his work. Until he was once more vicariously with her, playing the same movie again, or a different one, examining her body in vivid detail, each and every part from ears to toes, finding with his tongue and his eyes, what he wanted between her legs, every school boy's fantasy as he imagined what she would look like there, his tongue teasing her open, Izzy by now wanton, wide, her beauty complete.

What he wrote was nothing like this, that would warrant a slap. He spoke of limbs and eyes and sometimes long necks and tender mouths. And then, in a moment of madness, in one of his later letters to her, he told her too how much he wanted her in his arms, how much he longed for her bare legs to be wrapped around him, how much he dreamed of burying his head between her legs and staying there for the rest of his life, how much he ached for her, so much so that sometimes he couldn't even stand up straight. In a further moment of madness, he posted it. And when it was gone, he spent the night vomiting, convinced that this would mean she would reject him as a chancer and a rogue and a vulgar one at that, not seeing the lovesick madman he had become.

In fact, this would be the letter that Izzy would read the most – over and over and over and over – trying to experience through her heartbreak that was now complete, the moment of consummation that they never had.

We have a fresh clue now that the fairy tale does not end well, but quite how savage and sudden, we don't yet know. So that we are not slain the way Izzy was, let's warn ourselves of what is soon to come. Izzy had no such warning and the shutters that came down all around her, came down all the more decisively for the brutal shock, guillotining all joy, barricading her in, steel upon steel, unreachable evermore.

CHAPTER 8

On the 13th of January, 14 days before they were due to be married and 13 days before Homi was due back from Lucknow, Ferangiz was on the train back from Bombay to Poona. She had been helping Mrs. Indrani with the wedding arrangements, together with Ruky, Chinni included as much as she could from a distance as she had to stay with Farida and by all accounts all the women were happy. Although Chinni persisted in feeling that she should have hosted the wedding, it was also a financial relief not to and nobody made her even for one moment feel that she had failed in her duty, nor did they even think it, and in her sweet way she went along with things. It was to be a small occasion, simple, held in the Indrani's own home, the largish apartment she had moved to after General Indrani died, with a blessing at the agiary – the fire temple of their Parsi faith – later.

Ferangiz could imagine being part of this family with their easy, unshowy ways and light touch to dogma and ceremony, but on the train back to Poona it was not the family she was thinking of but Homi. In her handbag a clutch of his letters, one held in her hand, each of them so well worn as to almost feel antiquated, the paper thumbed and thin, she filled with him, heady, the sway of the train only adding to it. She too felt the unbearable wait, the way Homi did. Her mind filled with shifting images of him, stored in vivid memory, like a card deck, or sensual Roladex that she flicked through over and over. Homi on his horse ahead of her, his dark hair wet at the base with the heat, his back rising and falling, his head turning back towards her smiling; Homi riding alongside her, glancing at her sideways in a way that she could instinctively feel, so that she too looked over at him; Homi bringing his horse alongside her, his arm reaching towards the small of her back, 'tilt here a little more Izzy, feel that? That's what you want, that will give you an easy rise,' his hand lingering a little longer than he needed to and Izzy wanting to freeze time, freeze it, so that his hand would forever be on her in that way; Homi breaking into a gallop, shouting, 'let go Izzy, let go, give yourself to the horse!' his confidence giving her confidence as she did, and the horse feeling it and lengthening its stride and Izzy's heart lurching with terror and then letting go, letting go and flying with him. Was she ever happier than in that moment? Flying along with Homi, their horses abreast, his confidence in her helping her find her own wings. This, *this* was what she was born for. The Roladex flew and there was Homi again his hand adjusting her feet by the saddle, cupping her heel, she aquiver from head to foot. She closed her eyes and over the clack of the train, heard his voice in her head saying her name, Izzy, Izzy, Izzy.

The train clattered over the Ghats, a precipitous drop on both sides, the ravines making the clattering louder still, and for a moment Ferangiz had a funny sensation run up her spine. She shook it off, she'd never had a head for heights and she returned to the letter in her hand, intentionally not looking out of the window at the steep fall, his words holding her steady, my dear sweet wild Izzy, my dear sweet wild Izzy, smiling as the Roladex threw in his claim that the first time they'd met was at Mrs. Chenoy's. 'Yes, Izzy, we were in the same room together, and just because you did not look my way does not mean we did not meet, on a quantum level we did,' knowing he had won as she couldn't argue with that.

Later, Ferangiz would wish she never had, that on a quantum level, or on a horse, or in spirit, or in flesh, that she had never laid eyes on Homi, but wait, wait we race again. Or perhaps the pain of the ending is too much, and it is best over with.

Ferangiz being born independent – if you believe such a thing, or whether it's life's circumstances that decree our proclivities – Ferangiz being independent had elected by prior arrangement to get a taxi home. 'Yes, ma, I will be fine, there is no point you coming all the way in a taxi yourself in the midday sun to collect me. It is safe Ma, these days. I've never had any trouble. The train arrives at 11.30 and I should be home, if it's on time, by 12.15 or so, ok?'

It was on time. She hailed a taxi outside the station, her blue valise by her side, oblivious of the beguiling picture she made, the tall girl with the single plait and the arresting eyes hailing a taxi all by herself, which despite her reassurances to her mother, was in those days in early 1960's India a singular act indeed. The taxis more or less bumped into each other as they jostled to be the one that would get to carry this striking cargo. She got in, her case on the seat next to her, winding the window down and settling back in the seat to continue her private reverie, with the streets of Poona passing unseen before her eyes. Arriving at Balthazar House, the driver leapt out to open the gates and drive her in but she stopped him, 'it's quite alright,' leaning forward to pay him and then carrying her suitcase in. Absence might make the heart grow fonder and it certainly makes the eye keener. Izzy having not been away from home before, saw it with new eyes. She saw the crumbling plaster and the worn chiks, the way that other people must see it and it saddened her briefly, but then the familiar shade of the mango trees was upon her, Taxi the stray dog that they fed stirred from his siesta enough to absently wag his tail, her mother appeared on the verandah, running down the steps to greet her and she felt all at once happy to be home.

'How was it?' her mother bubbled, happy and relieved to have her daughter home safe, all Ferangiz's new-fangled ideas of getting taxis home by herself having worn her remaining nerves thin.

'The Indranis are wonderful, mama,' Ferangiz said, hugging her mother, Chinni trying not to gush at the pleasure of having her daughter embrace her. She knew she could never ever live up to the bond that the girl and her father had shared, a fact that always hurt making her feel ever inferior, but also deeply happy in the rare moments when Ferangiz reached across the chasm towards her. Perhaps this was the moment her mother would hang on to most, in the way that Ferangiz would hang on most to the moment when she and Homi galloped side by side, though there were many, many others in the Roladex that she would try to forget for many, many years to come. For now, this was Chinni's moment, her happy daughter in her embrace...before it happened, and their world stopped turning once more.

Inside, the phone rang. 'That must be Homi!' said Ferangiz, lighting up like a sparkler as she dropped her bag and ran inside. Phones did not ring often in those days, calls were expensive, people sent telegrams, there was no reason for Ferangiz to think it would be anyone else knowing Homi would have booked a trunk call to see she had got home safe. 'Hello?' she said slightly out of breath – and not just because she had charged to get to the phone – as the operator put the call through, 'Homi?'

There was a silence on the other end, not unusual with those old lines that crackled and snaffled making callers sound even further away than they really were. 'Hello? Homi?' said Ferangiz again.

'Hello, may I speak with Ferangiz Mistry?' a male voice, but one she didn't recognize.

'Yes, this is Ferangiz speaking.'

There was another silence. The line crackled. But that was definitely a silence no doubt.

'Yes, who is this please?' Ferangiz now somewhere between impatient and worried.

'Ferangiz, my name is Billy. I'm Homi's friend.'

A silence again.

'Is everything ok? Is Homi ok?' A sudden panic rising.

Another silence, accompanied by a snuffling sound, Ferangiz again unsure if it was the bad line.

'Ferangiz is there anyone with you? You are not on your own?'

'What's happened?'

The silence again.

'What's happened to Homi?' she was starting to scream

The snuffle turned into a kind of sob.

'Ferangiz, I don't know how to say this to you. Ferangiz, Homi was killed in an accident today. He fell from his horse. He's dead, Ferangiz, he's dead.'

The crackling line was filled with a single sound, a wailing crescendo of unreachable horror, as outside a rain started to fall, a torrent, a torrent. Even Kalina plummeting closer was unable to part the clouds and a grey shroud settled over the earth.

CHAPTER 9

When Homi was asked to make a trip to the Jutogh Cantonment near Simla, he was at first annoyed. He had enough on his plate what with the regiment here in Lucknow and orchestrating the wedding as much as needed from afar, plus he had the considerable distraction of Izzy that was making him much less efficient than usual. Normally he would have jumped at the request, Kulri near Jutogh being one of his favourite places in the world, and it was only the hinted possibility that there might be need of him being there on a more permanent basis – which would mean a life in the pines for him and Izzy and an escape from the overcrowded dust pit that was Lucknow – that made him more amenable to the task.

There was only just over two weeks now to the wedding and he agreed to make the trip on the agreement that he could leave early for Bombay – even the army having to bend its own orders as if one can't be at one's own wedding then whose wedding can we be at.

It was an unseasonably cold winter with snow arriving heavily and early. Homi hoped this would not cause delays, thinking to himself that perhaps he should request to depart for Bombay even earlier to avoid any unexpected bad weather holdups. He had been posted to Jutogh for a brief period when he was a junior officer and he still knew some of the men there. Now that he had talked himself round, he was looking forward to it and to seeing his old buddies. He was also looking forward to a mountain hack even if he didn't have Alaska.

Given he was only there for a few days it was difficult to find the time to get out on the mountain and he asked the syce the night he arrived to have one of the horses saddled up for him early the next morning, so that he could be out with the rising sun and back comfortably in time for breakfast at the mess with the others. His old buddy Sodhi – a jovial Sikh officer – said he would join him. The two men met outside the stables at 6 am, steaming hot sweet tea in hand, a good couple of hours hack ahead of them. Homi was on a spirited young Marwari – a stallion called Raja – and Sodhi was on an older Marwari, a still speedy light-footed chestnut. They headed out of Juthog, eight nostrils fogging the freezing air. It had snowed overnight, and the mountains were hush, that particular sort of hush. There's nothing messy about clear winter days, thought Homi, breathing it in, even the way they sound.

Raja was a joy to ride, a little spirited, you had to watch him, but he was fit and responsive. They picked their way through the forest out on to the wider pass. Izzy would love this, thought Homi, this is where we should live, me and my girl. The men didn't talk much enjoying the silence but when they paused at the top of the pass Sodhi said to his friend, 'Billy tells me you're getting married, you old fox.' Homi grinned. 'Wait till you meet her, Sodhi.'

They headed down towards Kulri, Homi leading, Sodhi right on Raja's tail, picking up pace now, the horses trotting down the narrow pass. What followed happened so quickly that when Sodhi, still in shock, tried to recount it later, it was difficult for him to sequence what exactly had gone wrong. Had there been a bang? There were some rocks being detonated further down the mountain, but they were a ways off. Nevertheless, something had scared Raja. Best he could remember, Raja lost his footing, slipping on the edge of the mountain throwing Homi with him over on his side, then the horse scrambling up again, Homi's foot caught in the stirrup and unable to untangle himself skilled horseman though he was, getting dragged along by Raja who by now was bolting, Homi's head banging on the ground, still trying to raise himself by the strength of his stomach like a circus rider, oddly not screaming, silent, his head hitting a jagged rock under the snow, his skull splitting open, black hair parting into red blood, a trail of crimson spraying onto the white snow, Sodhi galloping, trying to catch Raja and stop him, which only served to spur him on until the pass turned sharply and Raja finally stopped, Homi, dangling from the stirrup over the edge of the mountain, eyes open in static horror, Sodhi jumping off to get to him, too late too late too late, Sodhi vomiting in a heap next to his head. And then the great Sikh crying into the hushed morning, his cry turning into an endless, echoing wail, over the pass and the silent ravines and the pines and the soft snow.

There's nothing messy about clear winter days. Even the way they sound.

.

Part Three

IZZY

CHAPTER 1

In some ways the greatest cruelty was that his letters continued to come, the post taking a good 15 days to make it across the plains, in the clanking trains, through the sleepy post offices and the postmen's siestas, most regarding it a minor miracle that the missives actually made it at all, with a good deal of them the truth be told not arriving at their hoped destination, regardless if you marked them 'Post Haste' or 'Par Avion' this last especially redundant there being no sign of an Avion in sight.

Perhaps the greater cruelty still, was that on the eve of what should have been their wedding, Homi's letter arrived – the one in which he described without shame how much he desired Ferangiz's body, the one in which he wrote how he wanted to spend his life with his head buried between her legs – her stricken hands reaching for it as her mother tearfully handed it to her after considerable prevarication, fretful that it would send her daughter over the edge into madness. As it was, Ferangiz would leave the letters unopened as they stacked up, arriving every three or four days for the two weeks or so after Homi's death.

Was leaving them so, her way of keeping him alive? That if there were still words he hadn't yet said to her, that she hadn't yet heard him say, then he was still in the wings and she was just as before simply awaiting his arrival. That if there were still words he hadn't yet said to her, that she hadn't heard him say yet, that the world would still be pregnant with him. Maybe it was this. Maybe it was that the once anticipated letters that had made her hands tremble in a different way as she checked the letterbox excitedly after college in the afternoons, now were a tombstone of loss under which she lay buried. Her world not quite pitch black, that would mean a kind of oblivion but instead a grey ghostly shift, in which people moved and words were uttered, but nothing was seen or fully heard, she existing behind a shroud, the world with all its colour, the sky with all its blue divorced to her, the tombstone pushing her down, down so she could barely breathe, the cold granite stone, merciless. Sometimes there was a blurred mist of hope on waking from the sleep she hadn't slept, before she realized no it wasn't a bad dream, the digging claw gripping her again, a twisted chain of torment that tightened around her and within which his sweet, wild Izzy atrophied.

She atrophied to survive it. She could have gone one of two ways. She could have taken a horse from the military stables, mounted it bareback and ridden, ridden it forever, riding out the grief, riding out the life together that had been taken from them, riding out the meaningless injustice of it all, she could have dug her spurs into herself, bloodletting the pain out, she could have let the wail buried within her lungs unfurl, hurling it out of her mouth in an expanding cry that would have shaken the heavens, she could have let the torment that occupied her every single cell out through her whipping hair, the wind snaking it up and away from her, cleansing, releasing, every trace of Homi washed from her body as she rode in the lashing rain, so that by the time she reached the edge of herself, she would arrive, panting, free.

She could have done this. And maybe if she had, or could have, her path through life would have been a different one, our lives being the sum total of the conscious or unconscious choices we make: whether we choose to act from love or fear, to tread on the worm or to tiptoe around it, to embrace our mothers and the sins of our fathers or to blame them forever amen, to turn towards the right fork in the road instead of the wrong one, whatever right or wrong may be – though our hearts always know – to lock our doors or open our minds, to phone home, to water our house-plants, to smell the roses, to walk kindly upon this earth while we are still here, to let our hearts break. Or not.

What Izzy chose, though she did not actively choose it, she did not consciously decide this is what I am going to do, was to simply revert to the only way she knew how. Her shutters came down. The steel grills that before had been her occasional defence became the solid steel doors of solitary confinement, no gaps to see her through or to look out from, save a food hatch that mostly had to be opened from the outside rather than within. Her walls went up in much the same way as they had when her father had died, except this time the walls were thicker and higher, the steel Sheffield, the rivets tight. She encased herself, the floor of her cell also metal, so that the warmth and give of the earth or its potential to quake and crack could not touch her. Her loping feet that had once worn a toe ring, had once padded barefoot around their orchard, that had once girdled a horse, that had once nuzzled a dog's ear, that had once been grazed by a blue sari that had caught the eye of a 26 year old lieutenant in a way that changed him forever, these feet became fixed and austere. If the lieutenant were to time travel forward and attend another party at Mrs. Chenoy's, these feet would no longer make him lurch forward to the point where he would almost topple over because these feet no longer belonged to the same person. Rapunzel retreated, pulling her lovely feet up into her tower away from the world. Izzy once more became Ferangiz, the pillar salted, the tears like a dam to a river, cut off and stopped.

Ruky, heartbroken in her brother's loss, reached out to Ferangiz, wanting in some way to share this grief, to somehow soothe it even if only briefly. But Ferangiz could not. She could not share this. She could not throw her arms around Ruky and sob. Ruky could not put it right. Ruky could not bring him back. All it would do would be to destroy her some more, seeing in Ruky's face his eyes, seeing in her brow her brother's, hearing in her intonations his voice. No. To have impressions of him, without him was the worst kind of torture. She had to cut off. Billy too, from many miles away reached out with his big heart to offer and seek comfort, calling long-distance from Lucknow even though he had never met her, extending some sort of living connection to Homi both for his heart and hers. But the familiar crackle of the phone line that had once heralded Homi's voice all the way from Lucknow, saying 'Hello my Izzy' was too much for her, plus a crackle and silence was now wired like a cattle rod into her memory. 'Billy,' she said, 'please don't call me. I'm sorry Billy, I can't.' As for Homi's mother, well let's just say she became unreachable to everyone too. And so the severance was complete.

The guillotine did not come down cleanly or the walls go up without mess or detonation though. The pendulum had to swing this way and that a few times before it found its hard centre. Chinni tried the best she could to sense her daughter's needs and do her best by her, but when we try too hard we always mess up, and in her own distress for this terrible twist in her daughter's fate, Chinni read all the signals wrong and only served to agitate her daughter further. Or maybe it was simply that pain needs a scapegoat. When Chinni took away the blue valise putting it away in the storeroom, so that it would not be there to remind Ferangiz of that fateful journey back from Bombay,

Ferangiz noticed its absence at once and screamed, – 'where is my valise!' - sobbing uncontrollably while Chinni stood helpless, too scared to approach. She packed away Ferangiz's wedding sari – the one Ferangiz had chosen with the very light blue embroidered border beyond the traditional Parsi wedding white – folding it in tissue and putting it away in the bottom of her own cupboard so that Ferangiz would not chance upon it and be accidentally plunged into yet more anguish. But Ferangiz, who even through the shroud noticed everything to do with Homi, lashed out. 'Where is my wedding sari!' she cried. 'Where have you put it Ma!' Chinni hurriedly running to her room to get it, Farida cowering in the bedroom afraid of these tumultuous swings of emotions that were tearing their house down. Ferangiz took the sari from her and running to the kitchen, tears streaming down her face, took the shears from the drawer, slicing the garment, shredding it, Chinni also wailing, screaming at her to stop, Ferangiz cutting furiously, crazily, then collapsing once more on the floor, the shreds around her, lying sobbing in a sea of white and blue and Farida and Chinni eventually taking her to her bed, sweeping up the shards of her sari while at last, at last she slept.

And on occasion while Chinni wept quietly in her own bed at night, trying not to wake her dear Farida who had taken to sleeping next to her again as a form of mutual comfort, she would hear the racking sobs coming from Ferangiz's room, knowing that the best she could do for her daughter was to leave her be, which for Chinni took such an insurmountable effort that she found herself squeezing Farida, holding on to her so tight as one would a mast in a storm to keep her there.

Happiness can be shared it seems, or more accurately happiness *is* sharing. But grief, grief can only be endured alone.

CHAPTER 2

After days and days and months and months or years and years, it's impossible to know exactly when, as time froze into an ice sheet of endurance and the events we normally have to mark our journey – birthdays, boyfriends, celebrations – were altogether absent, the household settling into a kind of held breath, no one yet able to exhale or give themselves permission to carry on living again, the days and months and years an icy flat line over which everyone tiptoed, afraid that it would once again crack and they would all fall through it never able to clamber out again. At least this was how the rest of the household felt. Ferangiz did not notice. Her own experience of time was altogether changed, having to hold herself fiercely in the present, in the tiniest moment of presence, as both the past and the future had jaws that would swallow her whole.

Even so after days and days or months and months or years and years she was never quite sure, she tentatively reached forward towards the past in the form of the one pile of objects that no one, least of all she, had dared touch. Homi's unopened letters of which there were five, lay still, as still as his body had lain on the mountain edge. Untouched, dust gathered thickly on them. To Ferangiz they gradually took on the size and shape of the bed she had had in her father's study, a trick of the heart and of the eye, an ever-growing taunting mausoleum of her love. Eventually she could ignore them no longer and she walked over to the desk on which they were stacked. Picking them all up and then putting them down one at a time, she walked over to the door of her bedroom and locked it. Maybe to her, going near these felt like suicide, an act from which she did not want to be discovered or disturbed, or maybe it was akin to being alone with her lover, an act also which one would ideally not like anyone walking in on. As ever, it is impossible to define exactly what she felt, to neatly compartmentalize it as this or that, when in reality it is all things at all times, a kaleidoscopic shifting, that doesn't really care for our dissection.

She had intended to read just one. Maybe this gives us a clue – perhaps she was saving up her contact with him like a square of a chocolate bar – or maybe it was that she could only take one nail at a time, but there we go again trying to define it.

Let's not.

She slowly picked up the first, slit it open with her paper knife, one of the few possessions of her father's other than his encyclopaedias that she had personally claimed for her own. She thought her heart would stop, so much was it ramming and faltering inside her chest, then taking a breath, she withdrew the letter from the envelope, sitting there for some time, for quite some time, before she opened the page. My dear, sweet, wild Izzy, my dear sweet, wild Izzy, she read, and just like that the steel shutters and iron grills clattered to the ground, the walls crumbled and her heart gushed up through her like an ocean, he, filling her again, and for a while, for a little while, the golden liquid that had filled her fissures sprung once more, almost as if he was there, right there with her, holding her hand, touching her knee, looking into her eyes and she like a hungry cadaver coming to life, devouring letter after letter, abandoning the knife, ripping them open now, clutching him to her, the torrent now in full spate.

When she came to the last one, the one that Homi had posted and then spent the night vomiting about having sent, when she started to read that one, shocked with delayed pleasure, slayed by his ravishment, the young bride that never was abandoned herself to him, to his desire and her own, feeling his hands on her through hers, taking off her clothes like he wanted to, cupping her breasts in his hands, eyes closed, finding herself, shockingly wet, had she no shame, no she did not, she did not, she had no shame, she loved him and would have none, why should she, finding herself with violence, she gave herself to him. Over and over and over and over she read his letter, *that* letter, and together with him, she came, over and over and over and over, the pleasure blunting the pain, the pages starting to smell of her honeyed climaxes as she let him do as he willed, her every orifice his. She moaned, she gasped, she bucked, she came as if she was right there with him, wildly copulating, free. Above her noises there was a banging on the door. 'Ferangiz! What on earth is happening in there! Ferangiz! Are you ok? Open this door immediately!' Chinni outside her bedroom and Ferangiz crazed and uncaring, getting up from her bed, the sheets of letter paper strewn everywhere, opening the door, naked, the steam rising off her, beads of sweat on her upper lip, hair damp, swathed by the scent of sex, looking at her mother wordlessly, panting.

No one spoke of it. People could handle traditional grief whatever that is supposed to be, just about. You don't say much, or you wail, or you sob, you have a stiff brandy and wait for the stiff upper lip, you pull yourself together or put yourself together, you carry on. But the crazed filly that opened her bedroom door, looking like she had been ravaged by an army and smelling like a honey-soaked whore, no one knew quite what to do with *that*. Not even Ferangiz.

For a while, that was what she did. Not in quite the unbridled way as the first time, but for a while it was just her and that letter and her hands – meaning his head – between her legs. And for a while this kept the renewed pain away or replaced it temporarily with a different kind of sensation. But the cadaver was getting hungry for the real thing, Homi on the page was not enough for her, she wanted Homi in firm flesh and hot blood and hard member. She wanted to feel *his* hands not her own, she no longer wanted to imagine their union, she wanted to see and touch and feel, and be seen and touched and felt, she wanted to lie in bed after and have him hold her and for her to reach out and touch his dampened hair and for him to pull her close and wrap her around him as much as he wrapped himself around her and for her to sleep, her head on his chest which she could only imagine as she had never actually seen it or touched it. And since in Ferangiz's mind and heart, no one but Homi would do, there being only one king on a chessboard, there was only one thing for it and that was for the dampened letters to be folded permanently away and for the shutters to come down again.

This time with a finality.

Clang.

Clang.

CHAPTER 3

Even if there is no purpose to things, for us to make sense of our lives on this planet, it seems to help to point ourselves towards some sort of purposeful endeavour whatever that endeavour maybe. It doesn't really seem to matter what this is, given that is seemingly arbitrarily decided by ourselves – whether it's the accumulation of great wealth, or the surrender to great love, bringing up a brood, chasing nirvana through drugs or sex or meditation, creating great art or shit art, growing enviable or not-so-enviable tomatoes, marching for a cause or against one, or simply to love and be loved in return, that last one the least vaunted but perhaps once experienced the most prized – whatever it is, when we have a modicum of purpose it helps to gird our loins in a certain direction, channel our energy with intent and generally make us less prone to mawdling or wastreling and therefore by and large seems a good thing to attach ourselves to or talk ourselves into. There is another point of view on this, much hushed up, uttered by an ex-Buddhist monk who seemed to smile a lot and looked as if he'd discovered the secret to life – that is to have a good laugh and a good nap and a good meal – but this was quickly shut down as there was a fear that we would all become a society of happy layabout sybarites and nothing would ever get done. But let's not get waylaid by philosophy.

Ferangiz had always been a creature of purpose, wasting time to her the most abhorrent of sins, and she had right from when she was a little girl applied her mind to learning and understanding, and later her heart to loving and living. When the latter was swept from her, to bring her life somehow back – she was here and therefore had to live it, she wasn't going to kill herself even though she often wished she'd been dragged off the mountain with him – the best thing she could do to be able to carry on was to point herself once more at some sort of intentional pursuit. This could not be fabricated. It had to be intrinsically meaningful, true, something that her soul could buy into without feeling duped. And since Ferangiz had decided that her own life was essentially over, she also decided consciously or unconsciously, most likely the latter, to devote her life to helping young people make the most of themselves, unexpected events excepted. Though she probably wasn't aware of her subliminal motivations, this was also something she could control, this was something she could direct and better still this was something she could both purpose-fully control and reliably direct without exposing herself to any more detonation.

Safe in the armoured tank while others flew, she trained them to fly high, to fly with precision, to fly their best. And in the same way as when one goes into battle, whether offence or defence, one's attention is trained and keen, not looking anywhere but on target,

Ferangiz's attention became single pointed, no right no left, no uncomfortable infiltrations, certainly no distractions, she shut life out, she shut herself down, she trained her attention on her pupils and became one of the most exacting and gifted teachers Poona or even perhaps India had ever seen.

This was an easy move for her, a comfortable saddle, as Homi or not, Ferangiz was probably always destined to be a teacher, her childhood spent buried in encyclopaedias, her voracious mind questioning and fascinated, her track record in college second to none. First, First, First, First, First. Coupled with all this she had a natural drive for excellence, if something was worth doing then excellent was the only way to do it. What this also meant, in part because she had herself been on the receiving end of such belief and encouragement not only from her father but also from Homi, was that she had a natural belief in her students: they could do it if they applied themselves to it, if they were inventive in how they approached it, if they wanted to *badly* enough they could. To have the good fortune then to land in one of Ferangiz's classes be it Physics, Chemistry or Maths – Ferangiz did not teach Literature, dangerously littered as it was with the grenades of the Romantics – was to land into an environment of inspiration and encouragement.

This did not mean that you could expect cossetting. Far from it. Ferangiz expected *a lot*, she would not give to you if you did not give to it, but if you did, and

114

you did because that's the effect she had, she would endow in you a work ethic and a quality of enquiry that would have your brain doing acrobatics, in a way that made you delight in the workings of the universe, an otherwise dull text book transformed – but if and only if you turned up to the party with every single part of you engaged. Daydreaming was frowned upon, or if we are to say it how it really is, strictly banned in Ferangiz's classes and she demanded absolute, complete and full attention. In short, you better have your wits about you.

Ferangiz's results did not go unnoticed. Students who in previous years had been given up on as dullards, metamorphised under Ferangiz's instruction, if not to brilliance then certainly to the very good or the finely adequate. Dishevelled urchins, whose socks were around their ankles, or their ties straggly, were suddenly seen to pull up their socks into perfect white parapets, their ties double knotted, even their hair nicely oiled and double plaited, asking their mothers if their shirts could be ironed a little bit crisper, and their torn white belt replaced by a new one next month. The little rich kids, soon found out that they were not any different, that just because they had been born into the silver lined mansions of their wealthy mummies and daddies and were dropped off to school by chauffeurs instead of walking three miles like some of the others, in Ferangiz's class there was only one currency that counted. Dedication. Even an exceptional IQ was not vaunted, and a student or two who in previous years had been put on a pedestal because it so happened that they could work things out quicker or retain things longer or had a more natural facility for algebraic equations than the others, these students too found out that in Ferangiz's class it wasn't being the best that counted, it was being *your* best that did. If Ferangiz had any favourites – privately it's almost certain she had a softer spot for one or two – no one else would know about it, certainly not the favourites themselves. Comparison in Ferangiz's eyes was a curse, one of the singular causes of unhappiness and in her class she wanted each of these kids to know that they did not need to waste their emotional energies comparing themselves to the rest but instead to get on whole heartedly with making the absolute best of who they were and what they had, instead of worryingly looking over their shoulders.

She didn't do it for the money. I think we know that. But it is worth saying at this point that the teaching profession in India is shockingly underpaid. How is it that the custodians of our children are given so little when they play such a big role – good or bad – in the doorways to their lives? Society could do with a good spin and rinse on a fast cycle of a washing machine, be strung out on a line, old creases ironed out and start again box fresh. But Ferangiz would not appreciate this distraction in her class, so getting back to it, where were we?

Yes, Ferangiz did not do it for the money. And she was not short of offers. The private boarding schools in Kodi, in Dehradun, in Simla, approached her. Apart from anything else, the prospect of educating the over-privileged did not entice her as they already had so much, but also any tenuous temptation to do so was instantly quashed since all these schools were in the mountains. Ferangiz would never even look at a picture of a mountain, much less go near one, it being no coincidence that she turned down teaching geography along with literature, even though those multitudinous hours in the study with her father meant she could trace almost any terrain in her mind. No, she would remain within the gates of Balthazar and Science.

She was also approached with vast sums for private tuition. Please Miss Mistry will you take my daughter, Riya, she is just not getting her sums right. Please Miss Mistry would you be able to start a waiting list, my Bunty will be turning 14 in two years, and she needs someone exactly like you to prepare her for her ICSE exam. Miss Mistry, whatever your family needs, we will provide for you, gas connection, driver, car, you just say Miss Mistry and we will give it to you for life, if you will just say yes Miss Mistry and take our daughter Neetu for tuitions, she is clever, we know with you she will be genius, please Miss Mistry. But Ferangiz was clear. Tuitions were for the kids in her class who needed a little extra help. Period.

The charge was the standard tuition rate, a paltry 50 rupees per hour, the same for each child regardless of their economic standing, except for those who might struggle with that for whom Ferangiz would quietly waive the charge. Some of the kids would get a little jealous of the ones who were selected for extra tuition, every single one of them loving whatever attention from her they could scrape and some of them even intentionally doing badly in class so that they could join the afternoon tuition session. Ferangiz grew wise to this pretty quickly and the kids got a dressing down they would not forget in a hurry, but in the end, Ferangiz softened and every day one kid who didn't need it was allowed to join the tuition so that by the end of two months, all the kids had got a turn.

The school in which Ferangiz taught, slowly got a reputation, with parents fighting to get their children admitted in their elementary years so they would be well established in the school and get a guaranteed line to Ferangiz when they were older. It was the school who was proudly and increasingly mercenarily aware of all this clamour, Ferangiz as ever was not. She simply got on with the business of teaching, walking to and from the school every day, her long feet purposeful, spending the afternoons tutoring the children, marking their books afterwards with her tea and then in the evenings reading some scientific volume or journal or the newspaper before dinner, eaten quietly with Chinni and Farida and then turning out the light.

Everything ordered. Contained. Controlled.

There was just one little thing she didn't tell people about. At least not initially. You see, Ferangiz, despite ordering things, despite focusing her attention on the children, despite latching on in relief to the surety that science provided, could not entirely let it go, could not fully cordon it off. And that was because she just could not make sense of it all. Why had this happened? Why had this happened to her? To her Homi? To her father? What had they done to warrant it? What had she done to deserve such a fate? What had the constellations of their families done to be so impacted, so savagely? Was it all just terrifyingly random? All of us merely vibrating particles in the cosmos, our trials and tribulations meaningless? It was hard not to hope for some grand pattern to it all.

Ferangiz had been brought up a Parsi and she was glad of that. It was a gentle order, not a warring one, you had to be born a Parsi, so unlike the fundamental factions of many religions, Parsis were not burdened with a duty or desire to convince, convert, segregate or obliterate the rest of the masses. They simply observed their faith, got on with it devotedly and quietly, and merged like sugar with all that surrounded them, exactly as they had promised they would do when they fled Iran for the safety of Indian shores. They were also in the truest sense of the word upstanding citizens

– often doctors, lawyers, teachers, industrialists – conscious of the world they lived in, with altruistic wallets and a light tread. As a result one could hope for none more than a Parsi friend or neighbour who would more often than not be civilized, learned, gracious, and in case you didn't know it often eccentric with an infectious sense of fun and hysterical humour that would having you clutching your tummy and not because you'd eaten too much Dhansak at their very generous lunch. So Ferangiz, despite not particularly believing in Zarathustra speaking, was happy to have landed in a faith such as this, taking the best of it as a code to live by and privately ignoring the ritualistic rest. In terms of answers to the questions she was agonizingly asking herself, the Zend-Avesta – the Parsi holy book – gave her no particular answers and she found herself struggling for a foothold in the gods of understanding in which she vested so much, her mind and heart continuing to search for something she could settle on.

There were two things then that pointed her ship's prow towards the surprising and un-Ferangiz like waters that we shall discover in a bit. One was the recurring theme of 13. The other was the number 27.

Let's start with the first. We may remember that the day Homi died, was the 13th of January, 14 days before they were due to be married and 13 days before he was due to arrive in Bombay. Normally such statistics would not even cause a flicker across the windscreen of Ferangiz's consciousness, but since she was searching for any signs, any clues, any sense at all in the senselessness of everything, the 13 caught her attention like a gnat on a clean screen.

Are we to take it seriously? That the number 13 is bad luck? A curse even? What a load of nonsense. Everything we have attributed meaning to, we ourselves have attributed meaning to, including the gospel truth, for who wrote the gospels other than a more ancient version of us anyway. Still, since the 13th of January had been the most ill-fated day of her life so far, in the absence of something else to latch on to, Ferangiz latched onto it – or perhaps less of a latching on, that would imply too tight a grip for a gossamer inkling. More like a spider's web in which was caught a single tiny drop of dew. A thought then that would be easy to knock down or swipe away. That is, if were not for the fact, that it was swiftly followed by the dim flash of the number 27, turning the delicate web, into a stronger silk, slightly more enduring.

The situation of the 27's is this: Homi had made the passage from 26 to 27 years of age on the 15th of October, three months before he died. So far so unremarkable? Yes, except that somewhere in the dregs of her memory, in the usual college chitter chatter that young girls often like to occupy themselves with – quite naturally obsessed as they are with what will happen to them, who they will marry and where their lives will go – she remembered Kamal saying something about a lot of people dying soon after they turn 27, Kamal being into astrology by which what she really meant was she read her stars in Femina magazine. She had said that apparently this was to do with a phenomenon called The Saturn Return and Ferangiz had remembered trying not to look too scornful as Kamal wittered on about how it takes Saturn about 27 to 29 years to be back at the place it was when someone was born, the orbit of Saturn around the sun being about that and that this marked one full cycle in a person's life and was why so many people seemed to die or go through a big change like a marriage aged around 27, 28 or so. Ferangiz had privately rolled her eyes but for some reason it had stuck with her and now it came boomeranging back towards her, hitting her between the eyes as she realized with a tremorous horror that Homi had not only just turned 27 then but was also about to get married that year.

It's tempting for us retrospectively to get any facts to fit, so that we can have an explanation that we can run with, some sort of interpretation even an irrational one, for when the unfathomable happens, this being preferable to nothing at all. Perhaps we would be better off yielding to the randomness or mystery of it. Mystery however is not the word that Ferangiz would have used in this context, so let's not dare utter it in her presence. Her eyes turned towards the vaults of astrology and what it might be able to offer her, as she privately hung to the sides of the world like a cold swimming pool, shivering and unable to get in or get out.

To convince herself that this was a lens worth looking through – even in grief Ferangiz had standards – she temporarily christened it the Science (?) of Astrology and Numerology, including the question mark in her own internal rhetoric to reassure her alarmed self that she was neither accepting it as a science nor denying it but that she was simply open to curious enquiry.

As with all things, Ferangiz applied herself to it with rigour. She started with her encyclopaedias which perhaps unsurprisingly did not offer her very much beyond the broadest of explanation and definition. She checked the school library which again did not yield anything on the subject. Good, she thought, we cannot have these young minds believing in this sort of hocus pocus. She ventured next to the old bookshop on Moledina Road, where she did find a fair collection mostly Vedic, including one called 'Vault of the Heavens' and another 'Predictive Astrology – an Insight' as well as one specifically focusing on Saturn. She took them home almost furtively, thankful for the brown paper bag, tucking them under the scientific volumes in her study when she got back.

She took to reading them after dinner once Farida and her mother had gone to sleep, sitting up in bed, a ghostly figure, her book lit by the single light of the old metal green bedside lamp. As she read, she found herself sitting up straighter and straighter and straighter, the parallels between mathematics and what she was reading startling her and then startling her some more. Eventually she no longer read in bed but instead at her desk, the decamp to the writing table signifying an elevation in the status and seriousness of her endeavour.

Soon enough the bookshop on Moledina Road, could no longer serve her needs unless she risked exposure by asking them to order her in some more specialist titles. She decided she had no choice; it was either that or learning directly from an astrologer. Ferangiz had a deep distrust of these pundits who controlled the lives of most of India – births, deaths and marriages, house purchases (as well as sales, rentals and layout), the inaugural journeys of cars, trucks, scooters, bicycles, tricycles (new or not so new), business deals (or no deal), all other events (major or minor) and ceremonies of all kinds – and without whose counsel one was forever uncertain whether it was safe to breathe, sneeze or fart, having better consult the well fed pundit-shaped oracle first to check the auspicious outlook and paying a fat wad for the privilege of finding out that things were not looking good, sit tight, sit tight, don't move and wait for the good winds. So, she ordered the books.

She had been keeping a running list from the bibliographies of the volumes she was reading, noting them down and picking off two of these to order first from the bookshop. They took a while to come, not exactly being on the bestseller lists or even always in print. But old Mr. Joshi at the bookshop was eager to please, saying to Ferangiz with a harmless twinkle in his eye, maybe you will read my stars Miss Mistry; and Ferangiz fibbing for the first time in her life, found herself saying, 'These are not for me, Mr. Joshi.'

But they were, they were very much for her, as she started bit by bit, with every cumulative title that Mr. Joshi went to pains to locate for her – kind old Mr. Joshi even starting to give her recommendations of rare volumes he was coming across while doing so – to accumulate enough astrological knowledge to be ready to understand and eventually read an astrological chart.

In the memories that would stay with her forever, in addition to the ones we have already been privy to, one such that would find her palms sweaty, her skin clammy, her heart beating fast, was when she sat down on a Saturday evening after the others had gone to bed to draw Homi's chart. She didn't have his exact time of birth. It was difficult for her to ask Ruky for it, having not spoken to her for so long, she certainly could not ask Homi's mother, Billy wouldn't know – despite the pair's closeness Ferangiz somehow doubted he and Homi had exchanged their birth times – and since Homi had set the wedding date as the day he returned from Lucknow, his gauge being it was the soonest he could hold her in his arms, rather than when the priest dictated it should be, she couldn't ask the priest. So she would have to go on a broad average. If necessary, she would look for 7 blocks of time in 3-hour windows, but first she would see what using the traditional noon mean yielded.

She began. One cannot say from the outside what this was like for her. For her to take her compass and draw out the circle, to map out the planetary position and ruling houses that marked her beloved's birth. One cannot say what it was like for her to see in her mind's eye the sky that had shone down on him on his arrival in this world. To refer to and cross-check his ascendants and descendants, his ruling planets, to plot each of these across the arc of his life, forcing herself to not yet look for patterns, to just stay with the plotting so the picture of him emerged true without her being swayed by premature interpretation. One cannot say what it was like for her, once done, to sit back, sit back for a while, then take a deep breath and scan the chart for the sweep of his life. To see without doubt the moment of their meeting, the voluptuous planet Venus bursting on to the scene, just when he said, he had been right, Mrs. Chenoy's party *was* their first meeting. There it was no mistake – Venus sitting astride in powerful aspect. Her eyes and fingers rested there for a long, long while. Homi, she murmured, Homi. It might have been many hours that she sat there like that, her finger on the moment of their meeting – his version of it – as if by placing it there like a pause button on a cassette player, she could hold it there and stop it from spooling away. A grey then orange dawn started to appear before she moved on, her fingers tracing forward, such a short distance, a cruelly short distance to January, and though strictly speaking you can't and shouldn't use birth charts to predict death, rather as a guide to life, in retrospect there it was plain as day. The irony is such an aspect on a chart can mean two things: an end to a life that once was and the beginning of a new, a marriage or sudden fame, for example. Or an end to a life, full stop. Either there for the taking. The blue and white of the sari or the red and white of the snow. That's the way the dice rolled.

Red and White.

Full Stop. Full Stop.

The next night Scheherazade-like Ferangiz sat down again, once more picking up her compass and fixing the centre point, swinging the pencil round to make a perfect circle. Protractors came out to measure precise angles, degrees were marked, this time plotting out her own chart to see what it would tell. Not the future, Ferangiz was not interested in the future, not anymore. She wanted to know about the *past.* Would she be able to see Homi appear in her life the way she saw herself appear in his? Would she be able to see the devastation of his death in hers'? She found herself hoping for it. Hoping that it would all be vindicated here. That he would be written into her life, here on this paper, that she would not be denied him here too.

She need not have worried, for sure enough there it all was. Venus blazing across her path like a sunlit moon, a surge of energy accompanying it like a horse across the heavens. She smiled despite herself. It had happened. It wasn't all a dream. But she didn't sit smiling for very long. Thence to the horror of the day he died, not even a fingers width forward on the chart again, there was Saturn, marching across, trampling her uncaring, violently entering her 8th house, adjunct Venus, squaring her sun, laying a sickle shaped shadow over her like a grim reaper.

As she had the night before, she sat like that a long while. Eventually returning to the chart, she now traced her finger backwards, a good few fingers' widths this time, looking back to the day her father had died. This time there was Uranus, planet of the unexpected, conjunct her moon, her moon ruling the 8th house of death, spelling unexpected emotional news… and wait! There was Saturn squaring her sun, the sun in astrological terms representing the father.

There it had been. All along.

Ferangiz sat unmoving. When eventually the sun started to creep through the leaves of the trees in the orchard, she went out and sat on her verandah. She hadn't slept but she wasn't tired. She didn't know what to make of what she had seen and inside she felt oddly still. The morning was soft, it was early, maybe 4 or 5 am, the birds just stirring. The lightest of breezes lifted the delicate fronds of the neem, wafting them as if in water, a gentle current swaying them this way and that, the light of the sun peeking through like a dancing reflection. She watched the unseen air making itself known through its movement, nothing to see, the leaves wafting all the same. Is this what it is, she wondered, invisible forces propelling us, so that we think we are deciding, going this way or that, but in fact it's all happening *to* us. She felt a sudden lightness up her spine and through her, all at once porous, as if she was the air and then lest she get carried away by this, carried away yet again into another unknown land, she shook herself, coming squarely back to earth.

Well, she thought, rising with a sort of determination, at least there is a way to predict it all. It might be a mystery but at least we can see where the pieces fall, that much we can control, that much we can forecast, that much we can surely know. No more nasty surprises. And straightening the chair, and smoothing the doily, Ferangiz went indoors, picking up the papers and charts, stacking them together neatly before putting them away.

That moment, there, just then, marked the beginning of an initially private but then increasingly public second prong to Ferangiz's minor fame. The teacher would also become a teller, an accurate teller of fortunes. And in the afternoons, there would eventually, later, much later, after many years of study and many moons and turns around the sun, be a different line of seekers, this time not pupils but everyday people, wanting to know where their lives would go, Madam, Miss Mistry, Mistry Madam having a pinpoint accuracy and depth of interpretation that would bring people from far and near to lay their concerns and questions about their lives in her hands. Not yet, not yet, but to come.

CHAPTER 4

Lest we forget that Ferangiz was not the only star in this family constellation – though admittedly she had the greatest magnetic pull – the other planets circling around her had their own lives too. A few years after Homi's death, Farida got married, it happening by semi-arrangement to a harmless and kind but somewhat unmemorable man called Anosh Avari. The most memorable thing about Anosh was how extraordinarily hairy he was. Farida did not know as he never told her – they just didn't have those sorts of conversations, their exchanges relating mainly to whether the insurance had been paid and what to have for dinner – that his voice had broken when he was eleven years old and along with that had arrived a copious amount of facial hair that no amount of razors, not even Wilkinson Swords, could keep in check. Consequently, Anosh had achieved a sort of legendary status in school, the boys in his class asking him a continuous stream of inane questions just so they could hear him speak in that premature baritone. which never failed to have them open their downy mouths in a cruel mix of both shock and laughter; three or four long years of that leaving Anosh with a lifelong desire to shrink quietly into the background where he would be unremarked upon, and in this he largely succeeded, except for his hirsute appearance which was difficult to ignore. He was otherwise not a bad looking man – shortish, stocky, not thin, not fat, size 8 feet, kind of compact, steady and unknockoverable.

He had learned to make the best of what he had and also to navigate his wardrobe so that it worked *for* him not against. He was known to always wear long sleeve shirts even in the blazing midsummer, and even then, through the cuffs and over his collar, thick black hairs would tuft out despite all his efforts to stuff them back in. Nature being cruel and always wanting the last laugh, by the time he was about 27 he started to lose the hair on his head, so that come age 30 there was not one, no, not one, that would interrupt the shiny round landscape of his shiny round head. He kept his moustache in trim, this taking dedicated effort having to clip it along with his nostril hairs both morning and night, a routine he combined with brushing his teeth, meaning that if you wanted to get to work or to bed early you better get into the bathroom before Anosh.

They had decided to live at Balthazar House, an unusual move as typically the woman would always move to the man's home, but Anosh's parents' place was modest, the young couple couldn't yet afford their own, and it made sense to simply stay at Balthazar, which though old and crumbling was a sprawling mansion not short on space. There was some debate as to whether they should re-open the upstairs quarters – their mother Chinni being against it, 'How will we afford the upkeep, especially when you are just starting out in life, save your money children,' and Ferangiz being all for it, the thought of being crowded out on the downstairs floor not particularly enticing to her though that is not what she said, what she said was it's important to be independent, which was also true, many a marriage going wrong or feeling quickly claustrophobic as people simply didn't have enough personal space and over-familiarity bringing out the worst in us.

In the end it was decided to open the upstairs, Ferangiz had a point and besides the couple did like the idea of having their own self-contained apartment. A compromise situation was agreed upon where they would only keep two rooms running – a bedroom and a lounge, at least until they had children – and that they would all eat together as a family downstairs as well as share the downstairs bathroom. This last, they all later discovered once privy to Anosh's toilette, was not the best strategy, but getting the water switched on again upstairs would require a replacement of pipes and no one wanted to spend on that immediately. The solid floors upstairs also meant that thankfully no sounds of the couples nuptials drifted downwards, though on meeting them it was hard to not immediately imagine what this would look like: Anosh with his carpet of fur and Farida with her smooth, plump alabaster skin bringing to mind a quaking thatched white cottage or a nest with a wobbly egg in it, depending on who was on top.

Regardless of our irreverent imaginings, they bumbled along together sweetly enough, he being a good pliant man and she a good somewhat pliant woman, neither demanding or wanting too much from life and quite content to peaceably exist, Balthazar House too enjoying their peaceable, comfortable presence. At some point in all of this, Chinni passed away, she had been getting increasingly frail and started to suffer from diabetes, a possible overflow from a lifetime of sweetness. She had never quite recovered from Ferangiz's tragedy or even from her husband Bhoman's death, the former causing her the more distress as she felt she had somehow failed her daughter, especially as Ferangiz point-blank refused to entertain the idea of any other suitors despite a queue of them lining up hopefully outside the gate. Chinni did not live to meet her grandchildren or they her and in this too her business felt unfinished, but she went peacefully and painlessly at home in her sleep as she deserved to, having never caused anyone any trouble in her life, sweetly going along with things so that everyone else could be happy.

The house did not feel too empty for too long however, though both young women missed their mother, as Anosh's and Farida's copulations at last paid off, a hairy squat sperm winging its way in a hurry towards a plump alabaster ovum and in that miracle of biology another very special miracle occurred. Somehow in that mix of pliant DNA, by some concoction of nature, there arrived at about or exactly 5.30 in the morning of March 21, 1968 along with the golden sun, a curly haired baby girl, a plump little baby girl who lit up the delivery room and thence the driveway and thence the entire house at Balthazar and the hearts of all who lived there, a little baby girl who was neither pliant, nor grizzly, but an irresistible little package of cheerful hands and enthusiastic feet.

A little irresistible package, that they would call Mehnaz.

And once more, life at Balthazar House would never be the same again.

Even Kalina, the majestic raven busy with spring far, far above, gave a little chirrup at the baby's arrival. And amongst us we might agree that that was a most un-Kalina-like thing to do.

Part Four

FARIDA

CHAPTER 1

The lure of chapatis coupled with the considerable allure of Mehnaz, had Manoj turning up at Balthazar House, if not every night after that first dinner, then certainly most nights. The accurate count would be four out of the six nights that he had left in Poona before he was due to return to Delhi. Suddenly things in Poona were looking up. His eyelids that had been getting heavy at the thought of night after night in a hotel room alone, not even Priti and her ministrations around to spice things up, his colleagues in Poona – a rather sober lot to say the least – neglecting to ask him over for drinks or dinner. Manoj, fond of any kind of sybaritic pleasure and always ready for diversion had wondered how he would ever make it to the end of this trip without keeling over with boredom in the evenings, now felt stirred and once more enlivened. The mother-maiden had pretty much been in his thoughts since colliding with her outside the gates of her house. He could still feel the buoyant weight of her breasts against him even though they had been there only for a glancing moment, as well as the curve of her rump in front of him as he had reached with her for the clasp of the gate. In fact, it was primarily these two thoughts that had occupied his mind and groin in a kind of never-ending circular loop ever since.

There was something about this Mehnaz Avari. He could not put his finger on it. It was not that she was stunningly beautiful and God knows he had been with a fair few stunning women in his time, though she was attractive no doubt, in a plump, touchable, very touchable way. She was the sort of woman, he thought, who just seemed to invite contact without actually ever doing so, finding himself wanting to curl towards her and pull her in, clothed or unclothed, sitting, standing or in passing, any which way just to be in communion, though this might imply a spiritual union which is not quite what we are talking about here. Sandwiched among the two thought loops, was that third impression of how she had turned towards him, at once surrendering – and yet not – to his near scandalous advance without a trace of coquettishness. She was completely without guile, with a kind of sensual innocence, no, it wasn't quite innocence, a natural womanliness, yes maybe that was it, a naturalness he had not encountered before. Was it that? Maybe. She seemed to have an indefinable effect on his nerve endings, every single one of them electrified in a state of heightened erotic charge, simultaneously lit up by a soft nurturing lustre that had him at the same time feeling as though he was being rocked in a crib by candlelight. What on earth was he to do with it.

However his words failed to describe his feelings, however his finger circled and circled but failed to hit the defining spot, one thing was certain. Manoj was certainly going back for more chapatis. Mehnaz's mother was delighted. 'Yes, beta, of course you must come over and join us again this evening. We would be delighted to have you. Yes, absolutely 7.30 is perfect. Would you like chapatis again?' What he really would like was not the conversation, or the company, not even the chapatis these last being very, very good, but the walk to the gate with the mother-maiden afterwards. Naturally he said, 'I would love some chapatis, I miss home food so much,' which to be truthful he really did.

'Hema!' Farida shouted happily, coming off the phone, 'Hema, make chapatis again for dinner tonight. And mutton curry, we have the Delhi guest coming. No need for raita, curd is best with mutton, we will have the sweets today.' Raju was dispatched toute suite by Hema to buy the mutton, a little late in the day, it being best to buy the meat first thing in the morning, but what to do, madam was behaving strangely and even Hema who was known to largely ignore all happenings except those in her kitchen, every detail of which she controlled and ruled like a despot, could put two and two together and deduce that Farida madam was excitable and behaving haphazardly for reasons most likely concerning this Delhi boy. And that must mean one thing and one thing only, and that was that he was being lined up for Mehnaz. Hema frowned at this thought and without intending to or maybe with exactly that intention, put in slightly less onion, slightly less garlic, slightly altering the seasoning, cooking the goat a little longer, so that the curry turned out slightly tougher, slightly less fragrant, slightly more pungent, slightly less welcoming than her otherwise near perfect creations.

This time, Farida was not the only one who would be considering what to wear, though she was feeling a wee bit cross inside that still after all these years she didn't dare wear blue and white in front of Ferangiz, opting with the tiniest of resentments for the pink sari with the mauve border. Not much could make her feel resentful today though. That nice boy was coming back in a hurry, which could mean one thing and one thing only and that was that he found her Mehnu irresistible.

Mehnaz got home from college that evening about 6.45 pm to a mother who was trying not to look too excited, despite being stood outside on the porch waiting for her, trying to sound casual, saying 'Manoj is joining us for dinner again Mehnu,' and Mehnaz looking all at once shocked and feeling faint. 'What time Ma, what time is he coming?' and then rushing to her bedroom as unhurriedly as she could.

Mehnaz was not one to keep things close to her chest, but she was not yet ready to share this as she normally would, this thing that she did not know what it was. She pulled one sari then another out of the cupboard, holding them up against her and then flinging them on to the bed, finally in a panic choosing a casual-ish georgette salwar – I better not look as if I've made too much of an effort she thought, knowing all the same that she did look good in this outfit or so she'd been told. She rushed to the bathroom, hurriedly filling the bucket, no time to put the geyser on, a cold bath was probably what she needed to cool herself down, throwing the water over herself hurriedly, a flurry of soap. Back already, *so* quickly? Her heart delighted in this as much as it clattered wildly, having her flush a million different shifting shades of red and pink like a rosy aurora borealis. She flew into her salwar and then brushing her wavy brown hair, she forced herself to take a deep breath, then another, then another. Calm down, Mehnaz, calm down. He's just coming for chapatis, that's what he said. She looked at herself in the mirror, brown eyes meeting her own. Hold steady, hold steady, she said to her reflection, just as she heard the gate clang outside, all steadiness evaporating at the sound, her heart jerking, her limbs turning to floppy boneless appendages. And at the same time, with a different sort of clang, she realized she hadn't said hello to Izzy Aunty on the way in.

CHAPTER 2

Farida had had to broach the news to Ferangiz that Manoj was coming to dinner again and she was looking forward to it even less than the last time. Ferangiz's wordless exit at the end of the evening yesterday had naturally not escaped Farida's notice, a tiny anger arising in her at the time. How dare Ferangiz spoil things by making a silent scene? Was there nothing she would not overbear? Close partner to her anger was fear, knowing that an altercation of sorts would doubtlessly lie ahead, and an altercation with Ferangiz was not for the faint or even the lion-hearted, lacerating as it could be. Farida simply did not feel equipped. Another fire rose in her, this time directed at an absent Anosh, why did you have to die and leave me to handle this all by myself, Anosh?

Anosh, despite his name meaning 'the immortal one', had ignored his nomenclature and died when Mehnaz was six, Shanaz was four and Almaz still just a little baby. He died apparently suddenly of a brain haemorrhage that was in fact a long time coming, the post-mortem showing a tapeworm the length of the Grand Trunk Road growing in his brain, that was later through a labyrinth of forensics linked to an overconsumption of pork sausages from a respectable Poona supplier whose sources turned out not to be so respectable or hygienic – or that was Ferangiz's theory anyway. Whatever the source of infection the fact remained that Anosh had had a worm growing in his sweet shiny round head for *years*, it insidiously helping itself to what it needed while being careful to keep Anosh oblivious and alive, the worm then either overextending itself or getting greedy and munching more than it should have, resulting in a sudden and massive haemorrhage while he was making amorous soundless love to his wife, his physiological combination of a bald head and hirsuteness contributing to a quiet male virility that needed to be regularly fed, feeling giddy, stumbling off her and collapsing naked but for his coat of hair in the upstairs bathroom, which by then they had got plumbed to allow for their ablutions and the happy bath times of their three little girls.

Farida later found herself unable to admit to her friends how he had died – both in what circumstances and what of. She did not even tell Ferangiz that he had died or started to die on top of her, though it's uncertain whether this was because she was embarrassed to admit to actually fornicating or was sensitive to the fact that Ferangiz never had, both possibly being true. Either way, she simply said she had found Anosh collapsed in the bathroom. She never told any of her friends that he had died of a tapeworm least of all one caught from a pig, it being only human to want to live and die valiantly. Only she, Ferangiz and the family physician Dr Wadia knew, not even the girls being told. All this makes her reaction sound clinical and pre-meditated which it wasn't, Farida was as distraught as her mother had been when Bhoman had died, striking her like a daggered curse and she vowed to herself with a surprising hidden steeliness that was not often seen under her sugary exterior, that none of her daughters were going to befall the same fate. This old house is cursed, first mummy, next Ferangiz, now me! I'll be damned if any of my babies are going to have their lives ruined in this way, they are going to marry and live far away from here, out of this house and even out of this faith where this jinxed sorcery can't get them. Emboldened by this trajectory of memory but mentally lamenting Anosh all the same, she resolved to not be drawn by Ferangiz or at least not be terrified and to hold firm. Hold firm.

She had not seen Ferangiz since last night and for the second day running found herself waiting with dread, despite her self-pep talk, for Ferangiz's tuition students to leave. This time she had no sweets as either placation or a ruse though Ferangiz was implacable at the best of times and certainly not lured by sweetening or bribes of any kind. She'd have to come clean. Being straight up was not Farida's strongest suit. Sooner or later, life brings us all face to face with whatever we shy away from – that possibly seeming to be the point – and so here she was having to go cold turkey, to the cold face, straight to the hot point.

Farida stood stiff with foreboding. Reminding herself again of her rallying cry on behalf of her daughters she steeled herself and set forth. She went around the side of the house, keeping her legs moving despite their contrary instincts, turning the corner and coming into sight of Ferangiz's verandah. Ferangiz was sat there as usual marking her books. There was no turning back now, Ferangiz never missed a thing and she had probably caught sight of her out of the corner of her eye. Farida went up the couple of steps to the verandah, immediately saying in as steady a voice as she could manage, her well-rehearsed lines: 'Ferangiz, just to let you know that Manoj will be joining us for dinner again. He called to ask if he could come by for some more home cooking.'

Ferangiz did not look up.

'I see.'

Farida not quite knowing what to do, but rather than prudently leave having delivered her message, she reverted to type and attempted to soften things, 'Hema, is making mutton curry.'

'Fitting for a lamb to the slaughter' said Ferangiz quietly

'Ferangiz, what on earth do you mean?' Farida's own temper rising.

'You know exactly what I mean. I cannot have any part in this nonsense. I will not be joining for dinner.'

Before Farida could say a thing in response or retort, Ferangiz got up, picked up her books and went inside to her study. She did not slam the door but she may as well have, as the reverberating waves of her fury, shook the atmosphere, like the seismic after-shock of an angry, earth.

CHAPTER 3

It could not have gone worse then, but for the short term, the immediate short term, Farida felt relieved. This meant that they could all sit down to dinner without Ferangiz intimidating Manoj with her icy politeness and sabotaging the proceedings. Ferangiz would never be directly rude to guests, that much Farida did know, but having her there especially in the mood she was in would have everyone on edge. She would speak with Ferangiz later, she thought, let the two youngsters develop a relationship first, let's see if they like each other before fighting this fight, she feeling quite the tactician. A deeper part of her suspected she was not really being a tactician of any sort but simply putting off the showdown for later, but she believed what she needed to for now.

So it was with genuine excitement that when Mehnaz got back from college, she gave her the news of Manoj's keen return to the family dining table, looking closely for her daughter's reaction should her judgment be off the mark about the sparks in the air last night. She needn't have feared. A dozing anteater could have interpreted Mehnaz's reaction accurately. Seeing Mehnaz's face flush, her eyes widen, then panic, then sparkle, all of those almost at once, rushing off to her bedroom to change, Farida felt a sudden tremor of fear. Had she done the right thing? She suddenly had a clearer sense that a train had started to hurtle, a train that she had engineered into motion was gathering speed, a train that might have no brakes or driver and maybe nobody, least of all she, could stop now. She shook the thought away, the way she was good at shaking away troubling thoughts, she looked around for her icing nozzle, yes, there it was and then calling out to Almaz, 'Almaz! Hurry up and get ready, we have the Delhi guest coming and go and find your sister!' sugaring over her discomfort as she stepped brightly and busily into the kitchen and asked Hema if the mutton was ready.

CHAPTER 4

The house didn't need a doorbell, the clang of the old metal gate was plenty enough and even if people used the little gate inset within it – which most did – the screech of its handle despite many a bodged half-hearted attempt by Raju to oil it, was so piercing as to be able to reach through the buried inner sanctums of pyramids in faraway Cairo and emerge undiminished the other side. But Manoj didn't consider himself the kind that entered through side-gates, plus he had a particular interest in reliving the reaching for the clasp – though that was probably not the best strategy for a respectable entrance. He entered. The women all heard the gate clang, particularly three of them, and each of these three had a very different lurch of the heart.

Farida's was one that contained the hope that all would go well, that the conversation would be smooth, civilized and easy, that Manoj's interest would be undoubted, that the mutton curry would be applauded, that the impressive young lawyer would see them for the fine family that they were, that he too would live up to her own desires for her Mehnu. And especially that Ferangiz would not make a last-minute appearance.

Mehnaz's contained a tremor of butterflies that fluttered with longing and anticipation, neither of which she could explain, but that had her adjust her hair just once more in the mirror, arranging her dupatta again, turning sideways to see what she looked like, what he would see, Mehnaz having the blessing of being comfortable in her skin even if it did not wrap a classically lissom package, her heart lurching at the thought of his presence, *here*, walking *right now* towards her down the Balthazar driveway.

In the right wing of the house, much more dimly lit than the main reception rooms Ferangiz's heart lurched too. It was comparable to the kind of lurch one could imagine one would feel if a train speeding at a 100 miles an hour, a train that someone else had set unbidden into motion, only to discover that it had no driver or brakes, raced it's way unstoppably towards the edge of a cliff, the tracks disintegrating, as the train and all its attendant carriages and passengers, no one spared, hurtled off the edge. She felt her breath constrict in her throat. She had to stop it. She *had* to.

CHAPTER 5

Mehnaz had resolved to not be quite so tongue-tied this evening, not wanting Manoj to think she was some kind of nitwit who didn't have an opinion or a funny tale or two to tell. She needn't have worried, as when nervous or anxious she had a particular habit of talking twenty to the dozen in a way that made her especially funny and entertaining. It was a weathervane that indicated reliably to those who knew her well, that something was up. So, despite the attraction between them being physically palpable, now that she was not so winded – thinking back to last night, it was almost like she'd been concussed – she was at her unintentionally entertaining best.

Manoj felt a little intimidated. He was the one who was used to holding the floor, relating the anecdotes, getting the laughs, and suddenly the mother-maiden had turned comedic and was unexpectedly doing just that. Nonetheless, accustomed to having to maintain a calm exterior in his profession, Manoj looked if not like a river swan, certainly a capable gondolier. You would never have known that he felt a little wobbly as he tried to commandeer the oars once more and steer the conversation his way. If he had sniffed that this was Mehnaz's way of coping with nerves, he would have relaxed immediately, letting the waters swirl, knowing that it was all for him after all. As it was, he had to be on his toes, his witty best, thrust into this female cloister that was turning out to be more like a bunch of lively viragos – the Mother Superior Aunt excepted.

They went into the dining room for dinner; Manoj, this time not making for the head of the table but to the same seat as the previous night as if he already had a position in this family. Almaz, also now emboldened – not that she needed much encouragement – was sizing him up quite openly, asking him if he preferred cats or dogs, as a general rule this being one of the ways she liked to assess people's character. Manoj who privately did not much care for any sort of animal, unless it was a juicy rump on his plate, hedged his bets by arguing admirably for both sides, considering he had no affection for either. Mehnaz was about to happily reveal hers with her story about Auto their adopted stray dog, who's name had the inconvenient side effect of beckoning an autorickshaw whenever they yelled for him, when she realized that Izzy Aunty had not yet come to the table.

Interrupting Almaz's chatter slightly sharply she said, 'Almaz, go find Izzy Aunty, let her know dinner is on the table.'

Almaz, was about to get up, but her mother, not entirely casually, said 'Ferangiz Aunty won't be joining us this evening.'

'Why ever not?' said Mehnaz, the tiniest of alarm bells going off.

'She's busy with some work,' said her mother, then quickly, 'Manoj, some papad?'

Mehnaz frowned but being tactful and knowing when to choose her battles, she turned her attention ever so slightly less happily back towards Manoj.

In all this Hema came in bearing a tray upon which was a plate of fluffed basmati rice and a steaming tureen of mutton curry, slightly less fragrant than usual, Almaz's nostrils already suspiciously aloft on the wind. She disappeared to bring the chapatis, one by one, hot off the tawa, and when she came in with the next one, right behind her came Ferangiz.

'Izzy Aunty!' cried Mehnaz happily and not without some relief, 'You could come! Ma, said you had some work to finish.'

'I do,' said Ferangiz, not entirely untruthfully, she was indeed working on something, nodding in polite acknowledgement of Manoj's presence as he said hello without standing up. No manners, she thought, as she sat down.

Farida could feel her face getting hot. What was Ferangiz going to do, she was going to spoil everything, she just knew she was, and she tried to look calm as she said to Shanaz, 'Pass the mutton curry to Ferangiz Aunty.'

'It's not quite up to Hema's usual standard,' said Ferangiz as she passed the ladle under her nose on its way to her plate, Almaz chiming with agreement, her bonhomie somewhat diminished by the sudden see-sawing culinary standards. Farida relaxed a little as it seemed the conversation would be taking a more normal turn, also delighted that it had been flagged to Manoj that the food in this house was usually nicer than this. She would have to have a word with Hema, she thought, I don't know what's got into her.

Tonight unusually, Ferangiz appeared to take a bit of a back seat, Mehnaz back in full throttle now that Izzy Aunty was at the table, Manoj trying to keep up, Almaz never happier than when there were at least two conversations she could be interrupting, Shanaz sucking absently on a marrow bone, Hema coming in and out with a never ending stream of perfectly puffed rotis accompanied by homemade ghee that had been painstakingly stirred and strained into a golden clarity from the milk of the shiny buffalo that waddled daily down their lane. They all tucked in.

Actually, if we look closely, we would see that in fact they all didn't. Mehnaz hardly ate at all though there was food on her plate, another sure give-away of her nervous excitement, Ferangiz exercised her usual constraint, eating just enough and no more and Farida normally prone to third helpings – food, especially sweet food, being her solace in all life events good, middling or bad – held back, partly because she was still slightly on edge, knowing her sister well enough not to take her apparent relenting entirely at face value and partly because she did not want Manoj to think she was a glutton. The rest ate as usual. Almaz's appetite was as ever undiminished, this having only ever been interrupted once when she had typhoid. Shanaz, well, Shanaz was Shanaz. And Manoj helped himself to more chapatis and ghee.

Ferangiz having not said much all evening – but to her credit, Farida thought, having not been too frosty either – asked Almaz what she was going to do for her birthday this weekend and Almaz excitedly told her about the birthday party she was having on Saturday afternoon.

'Ma, what are we giving them for their return present?!'

'Almaz, now that you're going to be thirteen you don't need to give return presents anymore!' said her mother

'Yah it's official, you're all grown up, a proper teenager!' said Mehnaz grinning at her sister; then adding, 'I've really never understood about return presents, I mean our friends *want* to come over they don't need a present in return! Whoever started such a silly custom?'

'Maybe someone lonely who feels no one will come unless given something in return,' said Shanaz quietly, Mehnaz and Farida looking at her with concern wondering if that's how she felt, Shanaz oblivious, squinting down the hollow of her marrow bone.

Ferangiz turned her gaze to Manoj, and asked casually, so casually, with a lightness of touch that any ambassador to the state would have spent years trying to get within reaching distance of, how old he was, when was his birthday, Farida almost falling off her chair at this sudden interest and geniality.

Manoj, pleased to have some attention from Mother Superior and the conversation back in his direction, said 'I'm 29, ma'am, in fact on November 16th I'll be 30.'

'A seminal year,' replied Ferangiz rather enigmatically, handing her plate to Hema, excusing herself saying she had to get back to what she was doing.

'Won't you stay for sweets?' said Farida, overdoing it again.

Ferangiz's eyes rested silently on her sister, who squirmed on the cracked green leather of the old teak dining chair, and then wordlessly left the room.

CHAPTER 6

Walking to the gate at last, this time talking on their way, laughing together about Almaz's antics, a molecular hush started to descend on the pair, quieting their voices, so that by the time they reached the gate there was once more a charged silence. Manoj was slightly less confident as it was starting to dawn on him that this mother-maiden might be the real deal, chivalry taking the fore. Chivalry meaning kissing those lips that had never been kissed, gently, no tongues, choosing instead the yet untaken path of delayed gratification, tracing her lips with his fingers once more, pulling away as they started to quite on their own accord make their way down her neck, this time asking, 'Can I come back for more chapatis tomorrow?'

The evening that had started with a lurch in three different hearts so ended with a hum in four. But wait, let us not so easily sew that up with the same stitch. There was a good deal of nuance in that humming, perhaps warranting a closer listen.

Let's hear the first. When Farida climbed into bed that night – into the big empty four poster that had eventually been moved to the ground floor, when she, just like her mother before her had decided to close the upstairs after Anosh's death, this time with a finality that meant that at least in her lifetime none of them were going to have to do this again – when she climbed into the big four poster that had to be climbed into even at her age, the bed being almost 3 feet off the floor and Farida not being much more than 4 ft 11 from sole to crown, thinking again that she was far too old for this hoisting, she got into bed with a hum. A hum that sounded something like a car motor that was purring along, happy with the way the evening had gone, seeing her Mehnu so happy, so much fun around the table, Manoj proving himself to be bright and engaging, Hema outdoing herself on the rotis, though the mutton curry left something to be desired – the engine missing slightly on that thought – and even Ferangiz being by all accounts if not amenable, certainly civil. At this thought the engine's purr faltered, and underneath, a skilled mechanic would have heard the catch of something amiss, something that if ignored might cause the engine to splutter or misfire and come to a sudden halt at an inopportune moment on an important journey; so naturally Farida ignored it, turning over in bed, thanking her dear departed mother and even Anosh for sending along this nice Delhi boy and nodding off in the land of alabaster dreams.

Mehnaz in the room next door, floated into bed, switching off her light and lay in the dark, lit inside by a phosphorescence, a luminous coral floating in a blissful warm sea. She traced her fingers on her lips, closing her eyes, imagining him kissing her, her body starting to hum with a feeling that made her realise what all the movie love stories were really about, floating off eventually into an endless sea of phosphorescent love-lit stars.

Ferangiz was still awake. She sat at her writing table, lit by the single light of the old metal lamp, hunched over a sheet of white paper on which she was drawing two separate arcs. All fury and foreboding held at bay by the hum of activity, as she swung the compass around, cross-checking quadrants and times and dates, her attention intent on star-crossed evidence.

In a different part of Poona, in the air-conditioned comfort of the Imperial hotel, Manoj's dick hummed as he jerked at it. Yes, he thought, as he came over the hotel sheets, this Mehnaz Avari maybe the real deal. Then he turned over and fell asleep, his dick limp and soggy in his hand.

CHAPTER 7

The next day it was not her mother, but Mehnaz, who would say to Ferangiz that Manoj was coming to dinner again that evening. Mehnaz had got back from college earlier, knowing that he was coming and wanting to be able to help her mother and have a little more time to get ready, as well as to be able to say hello properly to her aunt. She busied herself alongside Hema in the kitchen, boiling the water for Izzy Aunty's tea, while Hema toiled over her star dish of aubergine and peanut sauce that everyone loved, making it on Farida Madam's for once timely instruction. Mehnaz took the tea over to the shady verandah, Ferangiz looking up as she saw her niece approach, her brow involuntarily softening, Mehnaz smiling happily at her, placing the tray on the table, pouring it for her aunt, and then as she handed it to her, saying, 'Izzy Aunty, Manoj is coming over again this evening!' saying it with a wholehearted delight that was yet a whisper, ever conscious of not disturbing her aunt's concentration especially at this time of day. Ferangiz took the cup from her, 'Sit down Mehnaz,' she said, and Mehnaz did, happily, even though she was in a rush, because that's how it was with them. So it was a particular kind of shadow that then cast across her face, when her aunt said to her, 'Mehnaz, I know you like this boy, but you are way too young, my child.'

When she thought it about later, Mehnaz wondered why she hadn't expected this. What kind of cotton wool naivete had she been wrapped in to even think, or rather to not immediately think, that Izzy Aunty would not immediately disapprove. How could she even for one moment have thought that Izzy Aunty – pioneering teacher and north star to many a girl who had joined India's emerging stage of stellar women – would endorse her very, young love.

But in that moment on the verandah when Izzy Aunty said it, it felt like someone had taken a sparkler from her hand and stamped on it.

'But Izzy Aunty, I think I really like him,' she whispered.

'I know. But if it is enduring then you can pick up on it later. For now, your studies are the most important thing.'

'I can still study,' said Mehnaz quietly.

'The boy lives in Delhi, Mehnaz. It would be different if he lived here. It will be too much of a distraction. Leave it and come back to it once you have finished, child.'

'But I have six more years before I finish doing my medicine.'

'Don't be distracted by the first man who walks through the door, Mehnaz. You are too good for that,' her tone shifting towards vehemence.

'It's not like that, Izzy Aunty.'

There was a pause and neither of them said anything.

'I think I'm falling in love with him…'

Ferangiz took a deep intake of breath. Outside by the gate Auto barked, running after some car in the lane, his bark eventually inaudible as he gave fearless chase around the corner, then coming back into hearing distance as he made his way back to his gate, taking up his post once more.

'You think you do, Mehnaz. And I understand. But at this stage in your life it's sheer foolishness. He's coming tonight, nothing can be done about that now, but that is all. Put a stop to it.'

And that, for anyone listening, was most definitely an order.

As a signal to her niece that the conversation was over, she picked up her pen and returned to her marking, though Mehnaz getting up quietly to walk away, did not see the pen tremble in her hands, nor

her put it down, staring into tremulous space as soon
as Mehnaz was out of view.

CHAPTER 8

In the shifting balance of forces, there is rarely –
contrary to our eternal pursuit of it – a state of equal
balance. Power tips this way and that, an Empire
rising and then falling; a tide rushing in then sucking
out; a birth, a death; a hunger, a surfeit; a desire, a
sating; top dog to doghouse. And so, despite the stony
weight in Mehnaz's stomach planted there by the
weighty opinion of her aunt – the weighty opinion of
her aunt in which Mehnaz placed so much sway —
there was another force washing over her and around
her, an undertow pulling her out to an unfamiliar sea,
the weighty stone in her stomach being reduced to a
large pebble in its wake, skeetering along occasionally,
scratching a worried tunnel in the sand, only to be
washed away again by the heady onslaught of Manoj
in her mind.

   While she awaited his arrival this third evening, she
did not do so with an entirely clear heart, crisscrossed as it was with the cold grey currents of her
aunt's disapproval, the thought of his soon-to-be-here
presence acting as a kind of buffer, a swirling
aquamarine eddy in which that pebble of

162

despondence could be temporarily drowned. When he came through the gate, his eyes fixing on her as she stood there on the verandah unabashedly waiting for him, her heart buffeted this way and that. She tried to steady herself. But it was no good. If there had been any tethering ropes pegging her to the ground, these came free, knots no use, tent poles even less, and her heart lifted and flew towards him.

Did this third dinner in a row mean he was wanting to claim her for his own, claim her in a more enduring way, in a way that his mother – in Delhi waiting for news, rubbing her padded elbows with apprehension and having more than her usual daily quota of ladoos – would have desired? Yes, maybe he was. Manoj found himself considering this very thought as he glanced at Mehnaz over dinner, thinking for the very first time in his life that maybe this girl was 'marriage-material'. Not that he was particularly looking to 'settle down' but he had over the years sampled many a fabric, rolling out the silks, organzas and the cottons, the cheap nylons and the grateful heavy handlooms, taking them in his hand, feeling their texture, the way they held up to the light, grading them, leaving them unfolded or crumpled, but not yet finding one that he might want to wrap over himself, over and over – not like we said, that he was especially looking. But here beside him at the table was this most unusual and exquisite weave, a Persian tapestry, soft to the touch, rich to the eye, shifting in the light, with depth and story and golden thread, not often found or fully known or easily bought, a treasure that would hang well in any home (or office) whether wall or floor and not give you carpet burns to boot. *This* was marriage-material.

You see, Manoj regarded himself as a cut above the rest, a diamond rather than a glass marble, the product most likely of a doting mother, who had made it her life's work to polish the apple of her eye, so much so that when he looked in the mirror, he shone back at himself like a 24 carat Golden Delicious. Top this off with being the only son of a wealthy industrialist – though Manoj was forever embarrassed that his father essentially made nuts and bolts, forgetting that it is nuts and bolts that hold things together – and the benefit of a privileged education and we get a fuller picture. Manoj desired not wealth, which he would forever have in plenty, but the finesse that, or so they say, money just can't buy. It wouldn't be fair to him to say he had pretensions, no. He absolutely fully believed that he was better than most and he simply sought the necessary props and accoutrements to fritter away the doubts of those who might not believe as much too. The first of these was to become a lawyer, to shed the self-imposed stigma of 'businessman'; although the corporations he would get off the hook for camouflaged crimes against humanity would be far dirtier than any steel factory his father had slaved in. He was a good lawyer no doubt, unencumbered by conscience, working hard to hear those sweet-sweet words, 'we only want Manoj Prabhakar on the case'. And to this reputation Manoj was well on his way. The second was to flatly refute his mother's incessant matchmaking attempts, considering it beneath him to have an arranged marriage, particularly to the kind of dripping-wealthy prospects she persisted in introducing him to, saying tersely to his mother, 'Ma, please stop this. When I find a girl, I will let you know.'

For Manoj this meant an intelligent girl, a girl of breeding, a girl who could hold her own (up to a point, so long as he was in command and the centre of attention), a girl you could take to the company dinner as much as out with your friends, a girl then who you instinctively knew was the real deal and needless to say was a knockout in the sack.

So when Manoj, settled proprietarily into the chair at the dinner table for the third evening running, shaken and stirred by her yet again, he may have very well decided, even if he hadn't fully admitted it to himself yet, that Mehnaz was exactly that. He'd have to play his cards right, he thought, charm the family some more, not least that Mother Superior, because maybe, he was increasingly feeling, this plump grape was one he wanted to pluck off the Poona branch and pop into his mouth for keeps.

CHAPTER 9

Even Manoj then, frowned slightly when Ferangiz did not appear at dinner that evening. He was not a good lawyer without reason and knew that a scene is set not just from what is present but what is absent. He had planned to be his charming and erudite best, sensing that the elderly lady held the house keys so to speak. To not have the aunt here then, was a little bit like turning up to a court case without the judge present. Rather rum.

Mehnaz, for her part, despite the weight rehousing in her stomach when she realised Izzy Aunty was not joining them for dinner, was guiltily relieved. She did not want Izzy Aunty coming in to tick Manoj off or banish him, which she knew under these circumstances despite her impeccable manners she was quite capable of doing. She wanted to speak to her aunt again at length, when she'd had a chance to think about things and to handle her aunt's objections in her own way. Besides her attention at this moment was held by the tantalizing distance between her and Manoj's hand, the sparks between them flying fast enough to reheat a passing chapati. Farida, buzzed around the pair like a happy bee, all appearances of trying to look casual dropped and her delight about how well they were getting on quite, quite plain to see. She too was relieved about Ferangiz's absence, she didn't think her nerves could take another such dinner with disapproval at the head, two in a row quite enough to send her blood pressure all over the place. They could all enjoy themselves without having to stand to attention she thought, knowing too, that this reprieve would be short-lived. For now, she could avoid the looming cowpat and buzz around the honeyed flowers instead.

When it was time for Manoj to leave and the two walked to the gate once more, this time Manoj taking her hand from the very first step down from the porch, losing no time to be in contact with her and losing no time once again in kissing her on the lips when they reached the gate, pulling her close to him, curving his arm behind her back, his hand resting daringly slightly lower than the small of it, 'Do you think your mother will let me take you out for dinner tomorrow?'

She looked up at him, leaning slightly back into the weight of his fingers, there it was again, the rush, "Ma, might,' she said, 'but Izzy Aunty is very strict. She won't approve.'

'Dinner here again then? I've only got two more days in Poona, I've got to see you,' he said, kissing her slowly.

Mehnaz knew as she lifted her face to his, that she was actively going against Izzy Aunty's instructions, she knew she was doing something that would inflame, that this would not only anger but hurt her aunt, she knew this, and she also knew that despite all this she was going to say, yes. Yes, please.

'Yes,' she said. 'Dinner here.'

It was done.

CHAPTER 10

She did not know how she was going to tell Izzy Aunty. She lay in bed that night tossing between the tide of Manoj and the impending crashing waves that breaking the news to her aunt would mean. Mehnaz, washed this way, crashing back, a sand particle in her shiny insides, though Izzy Aunty was much, much more than a sand particle, plus we all know the significance of a grain of sand in the life of a pearl. The opposing forces of love and love, one calling, the other warning, and of her own heart wanting to burst forth into her own life in her own way, hurled her this way and that. All night she flew along the crests, then tumbled along the bottom, tossed in the grit, up again, flying on crests of desire, drag netted back, Mehnaz waking the next morning from the sleep that never was, a Medusa, worn and hair-tossed from the night's torment.

Fortunately, Izzy Aunty always left earlier than she did, so she had time. Mehnaz was grateful for it. As she poured water over herself, the bucket bath before the day, the clear water clearing her mind as it always did, she thought over what she should do.

She did not want to involve her mother, this was between her and Izzy Aunty, and besides that would not go well. She was only too aware of the sibling dynamic between her mother and her aunt, as well as her mother's tendency to drama and panic, deciding that she would speak to Izzy Aunty as soon as she could get her on her own that afternoon. This might imply a decisive calm she didn't feel, but a decision was a decision, nonetheless.

As it was two things happened that meant she would not need to.

When the truth will out, the truth will out, as sooner or later it does, all manner of things conspiring to open the doors and widen the shutters to do so. Therefore when it does, there seems little point in rewinding back through time to berate ourselves or lament, to say if only we had done this, if only we hadn't said that, if only we'd opened our mouths or kept them shut – in Farida's case that last being more common. This afternoon was no different and she was to find herself once again slayed by her own verbal incontinence.

What happened was this. Manoj's mother Mrs. Prabhakar back in Delhi had not heard anything of the couples' meeting, of how it went, whether love was in the air, if her apple had found his pip so to speak, it having been decided to keep things low key and for everyone to stay well out of the way at least until Manoj left Poona for Delhi. A goose however will be a goose and this one had to have a gander. True to her nature, by day four, Mrs Prabhakar could stand it no longer and no amount of ladoos, sweet tea and cool air-conditioned air could allay the anxiety that she felt at not knowing. So at about or exactly 3.30 pm that afternoon, lying huffing on her bed, her belly tremoring skyward with each exasperated inhale and shuddering downwards with each sigh, ladoo crumbs falling on her chest as she munched between breaths, she found herself propping herself up on her round elbow, rolling on to her side, crumbs falling on the sheets as she reached for the phone while brushing them to the floor, her stout digits plunging into the holes and turning the dial, her memory holding the number as the plastic wheel swung forward and back. She held her breath.

By the miracle of modern man and his many extraordinary and excellent inventions – discounting the many unnecessary ones – the turning of the plastic wheel by the stout, anxious fingers in that Delhi bedroom translated its way through a confluence of physics and wires all the way across the great plateaus, over the wide grey rivers and dry tributaries, over the full and the hungry, over the riots and the prayers, winding through the empty Ghats, down the thronging lanes, over the minarets and the flat roofs, skimming the skinny cows and the smelly goats and the black buffalos, past the golden retrievers and the strays, tangling in the flaming branches of the gulmohars that shaded a certain tall metal gate and a certain drive-way, before arriving breathless in the cool, dark hallway of Balthazar House, the shrill ring of the phone no match for Mrs. Prabhakar's voice that trilled out despite herself when Farida answered, a little jolted from her thick nap, as nobody but nobody phones anybody but anybody in the stifling hot sun of an Indian mid-afternoon.

'Hello?' said Farida

'Hanh, may I speak with Farida please?'

'Mrs. Prabhakar?'

'Yah, it is. How are you?' And then without waiting for a reply or maybe talking over it because she just couldn't wait 'I was just wondering how it went with the children, yah. Did they get on?'

Now just because Farida had been witness to the electric storm that had been flashing in Balthazar – and especially at the dining table– since Manoj's arrival three nights ago, and just because her Mehnaz had not been the same since she had walked through that door with him, rosier and flushed and distracted, just because she had been privy to this, it did not make it any easier to keep it to herself. Farida was simply not built for self-sufficiency in the way that some people are not built to confide and having had to bottle it all in as well as to hide it from Ferangiz had not been easy. So it was as much a relief to her to hear Mrs. Prabhakar's trilling voice, as it was to let out her own.

What followed was a flood of excited babbling, both women layering excited shriek, upon excited shriek, Farida forgetting that no love had as yet been declared, no intentions announced, that she was actually supposed to be being casual with Mrs. Prabhakar, that she had not even spoken to Mehnaz about the young man and what he was saying to her when they walked to the gate, all this was forgotten as in a crescendo of pent-up happy hysteria, pent-up in both women for much longer than the past three days, pent-up in Farida since Anosh died, deciding that she would for once and for all have to unspring her daughters from this curse no matter what it took, and pent up in Mrs. Prabhakar who pictured her son marrying one of those terrible modern lawyer girls who would take her apple far, far from the tree, that's if he actually ever decided to get married at all.

Higher and higher they went like ecstatic, out-of-tune violins, whipping each other up into a shrieking duet until suddenly, quite suddenly one of the violins stopped playing, her bow falling out of her fingers and falling in slow motion, not unlike Kalina's feather that had rocked this way and that landing silently quill tip-first to earth, except the bow did not land silently but clattered to the hard floor, finally coming to rest, the sickened silence filled with the 'hello? hallo? haalo?' from Delhi.

Ferangiz was standing in the hallway door.

Had she come home early? Had she heard Farida on her way in and come to see what was going on? Had Farida got so carried away that all discretion was forgotten, her excited shrieking carrying all the way to Ferangiz's verandah round the other side of the house? To ask these questions is irrelevant as no one was actually asking them just yet. As we said when the truth will out the truth will out and here was its moment.

'I'll have to call you back. Yes. Bye.'

Replacing the phone in the receiver with a heavy clunk, her skin grey, her face shrimp pink, she stared up at her sister, at an immediate disadvantage at the low phone table, with Ferangiz taller than usual at the threshold of the door.

There was a silence.

Silences are almost never empty. In fact, if we listen closely enough, we will find that there is no such thing at all. Across this one, waves of anger met waves of fear, projected thoughts met unprepared protests, imminent consequence met unstated truth. Whoever speaks first whether in offence or defence determines the seat of power, sometimes won, sometimes lost. As yet, neither woman had said a word, but it was clear who had the spear before either had done so. Ferangiz's grey eyes had the ability to lower the temperature of a room and a sudden winter descended on the hallway of the house – not a white

Christmas either – across which icy winds would soon start to blow.

Farida's mouth that had just moments before been happily open, moving this way and that in smiles and shrieks and shouts of 'I know, can you believe it!' now formed a different shape of dismay. Nothing came out of it. At all.

It was Ferangiz who broke the silence. Not to make things easier. It was simply that she had been too replete with rage to speak. That rage now found its flame and the icy tundra turned not into a spring, but a forest fire, streaking across the room in white-hot angry leaps.

'How dare you do this!'

Farida started to protest, but Ferangiz cut her off.

'Don't even try to pretend Farida. I don't want to hear it. Are you completely out of your mind? How dare you do such a thing. Mehnaz is 19!!! Arranging a marriage?! And without consulting me on top of it!!'

'She's *my* daughter!'

'Oh, I see you own her now do you? She's your commodity is she? Well, let me inform you that she is not. This nonsense has to stop at once. Enough is enough. Tell that boy's mother – I'm assuming that's who you were babbling to – to find someone else for her upstart son. Our daughter is not for sale.'

We all have a fuse that if tripped sets us off, and this was Farida's.

174

'She is not *our* daughter!!! She is *mine*! I won't let Mehnaz's life be ruined staying in this house any longer than she has to, I don't want her to have the same fate as you and me! I want her married, out of this house, even out of this faith if necessary and to live somewhere as far from here as possible!'

'Oh God, please do not tell me that this is all in aid of some stupid superstition of yours? Farida if you want to exist in that silly head of yours, I expect you have no choice, but do not impose it on the rest of us, least of all Mehnaz!'

'But it's true! Dada died! And Homi died! And Anosh died! And all of us were left here, mummy and you and me, shrivelling up by ourselves in this house! I won't let that happen to Mehnaz! Or Shanaz or Almaz! And anyway it's too late now! Mehnaz has fallen for him.'

At this last, Ferangiz went ice cold.

'Well, we will just have to put a stop to that, won't we'

Farida, extraordinarily, held her stare.

'Her education comes first,' said Ferangiz icily 'once she's done, if she is still interested in this Manoj character then we can talk about it. But first she has to complete her medicine.'

'She can do that in Delhi. She can transfer from here and continue there.'

'Firstly Farida, the medical college in Poona is one of the best medical colleges in India, students come *from* Delhi to go there, though I know such a significant fact could easily escape you. Secondly, we are not living in the 1800's. It is 1988. Check the date. Women are women in their own right. Marriage is not the be all and end all of their existence. Our Mehnaz is a bright girl, a brilliant girl even, she is going to make an exceptional paediatrician and you are not about to get in the way of that with your silly superstitions. And besides she is simply too young to settle down with the first man she meets and that too to a jumped-up Delhi lawyer. I will simply not allow it.'

'You will not allow it? There you go again Ferangiz!' Farida shrilled, 'behaving as if you are the Prime Minister of India, deciding what will happen in this house as if you are the ruling party. I am sick of you lording it over the rest of us, marching around as if you know everything, as if your word is the ultimate command. And who are you to decide about love and marriage. Look at you! You are just a dried-up woman, who's been alone her whole life. At least I have children. And Mehnaz, is *my* child, *mine*.'

She took a breath in shock and already in regret that she had spoken to Ferangiz in this way. Why is that we say the most hurtful of things in such moments, things that we will regret saying forever and that no one will forget, least of all the person we have said them to.

Ferangiz had not become the woman that she was by keeling over at the first attack. Did it strike her to the bone? Yes. Did she reel from it? Not yet.

She steeled herself even more.

'First of all let me tell you, that you may have borne Mehnaz, you may have physically given birth to her, yes, but she has been brought up by both of us. Thank goodness, otherwise she might have turned into an even more syrupy version of you. And tell me, since we are on the subject of rearing, did you sit for hours with her while she did her homework? Did you help prepare her for her exams? Did you rush her to the hospital when she got meningitis? Did you make sure all her vaccinations were up to date? Did you instil in her the fibre that has made her into the kind of girl she is? No, you plaited her hair and you made her sashed dresses. And that is good, every mother should do that too, I suppose. But don't for one minute think she is just yours just because she is the product of you and Anosh's vile copulating!'

'I knew it! I knew you were jealous. And don't take my Anosh's name in vain!!'

'You asked for it. I'll tell you what Farida, if you want to settle this thing and find out who's *really* jealous, let's just ask Mehnaz. Who does she come and sit with? Who does she say hello to first, who does she bring tea for? Who does she go to when she wants advice? Let's ask her and then we'll know the true order of her affections.'

The white-hot rapier hit the mark. Farida was burnt and wounded, shrieking back, 'This time it doesn't matter what you think Ferangiz or even what I think because Mehnaz is going to decide. She is in love with that boy. And there is nothing even *you* can do about that!'

Ferangiz was still. She knew it was true. She knew it was true. She knew what Mehnaz was feeling because she had once felt it too.

Her tone shifted.

'That is as may be. But it is our responsibility Farida. We cannot just let her throw her life away like that'

'But why is it throwing away her life?! He's young and smart and successful, well-spoken, she can easily carry on her studies in Delhi. It should be a happy thing!'

'How is it a happy thing for us to lose our Mehnaz?! How is it a happy thing for her to live one thousand miles away where we will only see her once a year if that? Are you crazy? There are hundreds of young, smart, successful, well-spoken men right here in Poona – not that he meets all those criteria – can't you see that he's an arrogant upstart, Farida! He's not worthy of her. She'll always have men at her feet. You are selling her short! She's too young anyway! And besides I can tell you right now that she will be throwing her life away, it will not be a happy thing'

'Oh, the great Prime Minister has spoken and she knows everything. She is right and everyone else is wrong. Hail.' Farida was by now beyond caring what she said to Ferangiz. Things had gone so far anyway and if you're done for the gallows, well why hold back, why not throw your head right in.

'On this I am right,' said Ferangiz firmly.

'How is it that you are so sure! How can you predict what is going to happen! How do you know that this will not make Mehnaz the happiest girl in the world?!'

'I'll tell you why Farida. I'll tell you why. Because while you are so busy wasting your life and everyone else's occupying yourself with gossiping and chattering, making Hema's life a misery and not even managing to get Raju in line, some of us are actually doing things that matter. Above and beyond tutoring my students for decades including might I add, Mehnaz, I have also…' and at this Ferangiz hesitated … 'I have also been conducting a deep study into the Science of Astrology….' she hesitated again, '…initially with the view that it was a load of hocus-pocus, much to my surprise finding it is not. But I shouldn't need to convince you of that since you are given to baseless superstition. Anyway, over the years I have gone quite deep into it. So when you started orchestrating these meetings with your pitifully obvious intentions for Mehnaz, I took precautionary measures and looked it up.'

'Looked what up?' said Farida suspiciously, knowing her sister was about to blindside her with some irrefutable fact.

'I looked up the match of Mehnaz and Manoj.'

Farida gasped despite herself, wanting to know what Ferangiz had found.

'And?'

'Well, if they went through with this ridiculous tryst you have engineered into motion, it will end in tears. And it will not be Manoj crying.'

Farida looked stricken. The curse! 'You mean…?'

'No, not him, but he will kill our Mehnaz. Not literally, Farida, take that look off your face. He's not going to put her in a tandoori oven. But he will stamp all over her heart. She will not be happy. It will not last.'

There was a silence. For a moment, seeing the effect this had had Ferangiz looked triumphant. And there just in that fleeting look the tide turned again and Farida seeing it, felt the old anger at being smugly beaten again by her sister, and she shook her head with vehemence.

'I don't believe you! You are just making it up. We have not even heard you mention astrology and now suddenly you are a pundit saying you know what's going to happen when you don't even believe in such things! Don't think you can fool me, Ferangiz! Don't think you are going to win this way!'

'You silly woman,' the forest fire once more aflame, 'do you think I want to win?! This is not about winning, it's about Mehnaz!'

180

'You just want her to stay with you so you won't be lonely in your withered old age! You are not thinking of her at all!'

'How *dare* you.'

'It's true! Mehnaz can be happy and you are getting in her way! I suppose now you are going to be able to predict everything from now on and we are just going to have to believe you, now that you are an astrologer pundit on top of a teacher and a physicist and a biologist and God knows what else. I suppose you are going to say you can predict my blood pressure and when I am going to die!'

Farida was perennially worried about her blood pressure, concerned that she should not die before she had settled her three girls, this being another of her little dramas, although to look at her bustling and chattering form was to be fairly sure there was quite a lot of life left in her yet and if anything her incessant anxieties were shortening the lives of those around her.

'Please don't start with your silly imaginings again, Farida! No, I am not going to tell you when you're going to die, that would make our lives miserable while we wait. But thankfully I know exactly when I will and that will get me out of this neurotic menagerie once and for all!'

'Oh good, well please share it with me so I can look forward to it!' the war now descending into a schoolgirl cat fight.

At that – perhaps as providence's way of preventing them scratching each other's eyes out – the phone in the hallway rang for a second time that afternoon. The shrill ring of it jolted both women. They looked at the phone.

'Go on, pick it up,' Ferangiz's challenge, 'let's see which of the marriage party it's going to be now.'

Farida did, not without trepidation, hoping it would not be.

It was Manoj.

'Hello? Is that Farida Aunty?' Her heart did not know whether to sink or leap, it doing both, but nothing for her blood pressure which bucked all over the place.

'Yes, beta,' she said

'It's Manoj. Aunty, I won't be able to make dinner tonight, I'm going to be stuck at work very late. I have to work on the case.'

Farida's heart sank. Was he cooling off?

'Could I invite myself tomorrow night instead?'

Farida's heart lifted.

'Yes, beta of course!'

'Let Mehnaz know from me?'

'I will Manoj, I will. We will see you tomorrow.' And in a final act of defiance, she looked at Ferangiz, a victorious little smile appearing on her face as she replaced the phone in its cradle.

Ferangiz stood there for a moment looking at her, then turned on her long pale feet, now even whiter with toe-to-head rage, and walked out.

CHAPTER 11

When Mehnaz opened the Balthazar gates, returning from college that evening, her eyes went straight to the side as they always did, looking for the figure of her aunt. This evening, preparing as she was to go and talk to her, to say that she had not acted in defiance but in desire, to explain again her feelings, her eyes searched her out a little more anxiously and with more intention than usual. What she hadn't been expecting in her rehearsals of what to do and what to say was for Izzy Aunty not to be there *at all*. The verandah was empty.

Now to convey the significance of this, the only time in Mehnaz's nineteen-year-old life when she remembered Izzy Aunty not working on the side verandah in the late afternoon was once and once only, and that was when Maiji – her grandma, Izzy Aunty's mother – had died. She immediately knew something had happened.

Her first thought was for her mother, has something happened to mama! She knew all too well that her mother's capacity for stress or excitement was not high and with all the excitement and stress of Manoj's appearance, her mother had been more highly-strung than usual. Oh God, she thought, and breaking into a run, ran up the steps, into the hallway, shouting to Hema, 'where's ma?!' finding her mother in the lounge in the blue and white rocking chair.

'What's happened Mehnaz?!' her mother cried attempting to jump up but the chair came with her and she had to prise it off.

'Oh ma!' cried Mehnaz, 'you're ok! I thought something had happened! Izzy Aunty isn't on her verandah and I thought something had happened to you!'

At this Farida sank – or more accurately pushed herself – back down into the rocking chair. Since the row she had been trying to work out how best to tell Mehnaz about Ferangiz's reaction, knowing how much the girl worshipped her aunt. As we know, Farida's synapses tend to short circuit under pressure and she had been ricocheting anxiously from one possible tack to another without resolution, the chair rocking back and forth with her. Now with Mehnaz bursting in like this, it forced her for the third time this week to go straight to the point.

'We had a fight, Mehnu,' she said, and before she knew it, she had started to sob. The tension of having to battle for her girls single-handedly, the horrible fight with her sister that she knew neither could forget and would strain their relationship forever, the worry deep inside her that maybe in this too Ferangiz would be right and that Mehnaz would be unhappy and it would end in tears, all of that and everything else she had carried in her, the way we all carry things without even knowing we are until they just rise unexpectedly like a flash flood, all of that came pouring out in sobs and sputters, the blue rocking chair juddering with her, as Mehnaz perched on the tiny narrow arm of it steadying it with her weight, her arms going around her mother, pulling her in, as she sobbed and calmed, sobbed and calmed, sobbed and calmed.

'What happened, ma?' But Mehnaz knew.

'She's against Manoj. She doesn't want you to get married to him, Mehnu.'

Still holding her mother in her arms, she said, 'I know Ma, but you both are jumping the gun, there's no talk of marriage! I've only known him three days!!'

'He can't come for dinner tonight, he rang to say he's got to work on that case. But he's coming tomorrow,' her mother said looking at up at her, her cheeks still wet, Mehnaz relieved to know Manoj would still be coming.

'You like him, my Mehnu?'

'Yes ma, I do.'

'If he wants to marry you and you want to marry him, then you can my darling. I will handle your aunt, you just don't worry.'

Mehnaz shook her head, there it was, Farida sensed it, that fierce loyalty, 'Ma, we're hardly getting married! I'll talk to Izzy Aunty. I know she just wants the best for me. Just like you do.' Mehnaz hugged her mother and then rising, 'everything will work out, don't worry, ma, water finds its own level. Now, just rest.'

And then she went off to find her aunt.

CHAPTER 12

Mehnaz's brow was furrowed as she walked over to the side of the house in the gathering dusk, oblivious of the chattering birds and the other sounds of the evening. The verandah still lay empty. The old teak chair with the smooth worn handles and the green leather cushion, brighter round the outside, pale and cracking in the centre, the impression left despite her current absence, from days and days and months and months and years of years of holding her aunt's weight as she leaned forward to instruct, leaned back to listen, sat erect to dictate, her back at all times poker straight, her students jerking out of their slouches to respectfully mirror her. This evening though, there were no students sitting straight-backed and cross-legged on the verandah and no books for marking piled up on the table. Even the doily was missing, as if a signal that this evening there would be no tea. A stray leaf blew across the verandah, crisped from age and the sun, Mehnaz's hair lifting lightly across her face with the breeze. She coiled it in her fingers and tucked it back behind her ears.

Izzy Aunty's door was closed and inside through the old blurry glass panes, all looked dark. Mehnaz stepped quietly towards the door, not wanting to pry by looking through the panes but feeling increasingly perturbed. She knocked.

Silence.

Mehnaz waited. Was her aunt asleep?

She waited a few more moments, looking down at her feet, then knocked again.

'Izzy Aunty?' she said this time, knocking gently again.

Her eyes caught a movement inside and some moments later, Izzy Aunty's form gathered behind the glass panes and the door opened. Mehnaz was shocked by what she saw. Izzy Aunty, always so neat and perfectly turned out, her cotton saris crisp, her hair tightly plaited or bunned, her face always scrubbed and clear, looked dishevelled. Her sari was crumpled, her hair though still plaited had come loose, her face looked creased and drawn.

'Izzy Aunty, are you alright?' said Mehnaz

'Yes. I'm not feeling very well today, so have cancelled my lessons and am resting'

She went to close the door

'Wait, Izzy Aunty! What's the matter? You're never ill! I'm worried. Can I get you something?'

'No, I just need some peace and quiet.'

Mehnaz hesitated.

'I didn't mean to disobey you,' she whispered to her aunt through the doorway, looking wretched. 'It's just that he leaves in two days. I couldn't help it. I can't help it.'

'Please go Mehnaz,' said Ferangiz. And even though she did not raise her voice, she just said it matter-of-factly, Mehnaz knew she had been shut out. The door nudged and then was clunked shut.

Mehnaz stood there, fat tears rolling down her face. Inside, there was movement once again, Izzy Aunty's shape once more loomed through the glass and there was a screech of metal rings as she pulled the thin frayed green curtain across the frosty door.

CHAPTER 13

Manoj prepared for his final dinner at the Avari's. He had a spring in his step and not just because he was going to be seeing Mehnaz later. He'd concluded an excellent deal for his client. They'd shaken Manoj's hand, slapped him on the back, the more reserved joining their hands in a Namaste nodding happily, this is a far better result than we expected, thank you Mr Prabhakar, thank you very much Mr Prabhakar, Manoj trying to be humble though this did not come easily to him, especially as he felt his reputation take another leap skyward. His chest puffed, he smiled confidently, even his cock slightly stirred.

Back at the hotel, aglow with the glow of his own future, he threw his things into his bag. Thank God, I'm out of this one horse town tomorrow morning and back to Delhi! If it had not been for Mehnaz, he thought, I'd have quite literally died of boredom. The thrill of meeting the mother-maiden had also taken his performance at work up a notch, the way desiring and being desired can make us feel invincible, so he had much more to thank her for than she knew. Things packed and room swept more or less clean – barring his toothbrush, razor and change for tonight and the next morning – he was set. He stripped his clothes off and got into the shower. Manoj my man, he thought, as the hot water hit him, life is bloody good yaar. His cock stood up in proud agreement and Manoj had a quick and satisfying jerk off, spurting a great big M on the tiled wall in speedy conclusion. He'd needed that. Now he could think straight about the evening and the small matter of a certain Mehnaz Avari. When opportunity knocks, thought Manoj, open the gate. This was the maxim he lived by.

And so it transpired that when Manoj walked through the gates that last evening, while Hema flurried in the kitchen, Farida kept triumphant watch for his arrival, Mehnaz got ready with a heavy and a hopeful heart, Almaz's eyes bulged with teenage excitement and Shanaz drifted about, he had already decided what he would do. He walked in with such clear intent, he might as well have been a Mughal leading his army through the gates of a citadel, ready for conquest. Call it arrogance, call it haste, call it dashing, call it romantic, call it what you will – but we might all agree, that the move he would make very soon was a memorable one. And by all accounts a most un-Manoj- like thing to do.

Here's what happened.

At the dinner table – you'll notice we haven't mentioned Ferangiz, who once again did not join them that evening – Manoj waited until Hema had brought in the biryani, and then as Mehnaz passed it to him, right there in front of everyone, without so much as by-your-leave, as she passed him the biryani, he held onto her hand not letting it go, and then looking directly into her eyes, right there in front of the others, right there at the dining table, saying, 'Mehnaz, will you marry me?' smiling over at Farida 'if I have your permission, aunty?' and then looking back at Mehnaz.

You could have heard a chapati puff in the hot silence.

Everyone looked at him in shock. Mehnaz felt faint and who can blame her, Farida looked like she was about to hyperventilate and was unknowingly holding a chapati to her brow, Almaz's eyes spun like giant ferris wheels, Shanaz stopped humming for the second time that week and even Hema known to thunderously keep to her course no matter what, halted in the doorway together with the incoming rotis.

After some time, the still room rippled, Mehnaz's words falling into it, 'Yes. I have to finish my studies, but yes. Yes.'

CHAPTER 14

It fell upon Mehnaz to break the news to Izzy Aunty. Or rather she took it upon herself, as much as Farida abdicated it. Farida had gone up against The Fuhrer once and she was not up to it again, not in this lifetime. As were so many things in this household of women who had lived together such a long time, this was implicit. Her mother did not need to talk to her about it nor did Mehnaz need to say it to her mother and even though their reasons were different, Farida's being a fear of her sister and Mehnaz's being the love of her aunt, both women knew who'd be doing the talking on her verandah.

Since The Fight yesterday, Izzy Aunty had behaved as if nothing had happened, nothing was mentioned – but a barrier was up, no doubt. Everything was courteous and polite, too polite, but there was an edge to every exchange where there had not been one before, the exchanges too, minimal. Though this was a blanket treatment for the whole household, it was terribly hurtful to Mehnaz. It was a severance and she was bleeding.

When Mehnaz had heard herself saying yes, Yes, to Manoj, the night before, the caveat about her studies had been more for aunt than herself, quite prepared as she was to follow Manoj anywhere immediately, continuing her education wherever she went, a given. This caveat then was the card she held in her hand as she made her way to see her aunt, hoping nervously and fervently and desperately that Izzy Aunty would if nothing else give her a listening ear.

For a person of logic and reason Izzy Aunty could be so unreasonable! Mehnaz understood of course, she knew that her aunt was acting in her own best interest and if the tables were turned, she would probably do the same, but to not even listen to her, to not even let her speak, or hear her out! There were ways this could be made to work and for everyone to be happy! Mehnaz was as frustrated as she was upset. Could Izzy Aunty not see that Mehnaz had not been expecting this either? That she'd been blindsided? Could she not remember how it was for her with Homi Uncle? Agreeing to marry him in a mere six days and move to Lucknow of all places! Mehnaz shook her head fiercely to remind herself not to mention Homi Uncle, whatever you do, Mehnaz don't do that!

Izzy Aunty was reinstated in her chair on the verandah, looking as if she'd never left it. Mehnaz approached and settled down on the edge against the pillar where she often sat when talking to her aunt or when they simply read together in easy silence. She didn't say anything in greeting, sitting there quietly, letting Izzy Aunty know she was there and that she was not going anywhere.

Aunt and niece sat like that for a little while, Ferangiz reading or seemingly reading the newspaper;

Mehnaz looking out or seemingly looking out over the orchard; and to an outsider it would look a picture of relaxed contentment.

It was Mehnaz who spoke first.

'I didn't mean any of this to happen Izzy Aunty, I can't bear that you're angry with me, please can we talk...'

Ferangiz did not reply, but she didn't turn the page of her newspaper either.

There was a silence again. Mehnaz's heart in somersaults. She had to speak, she had to speak, she had to speak *now*, she had to tell her.

'Izzy Aunty,' Mehnaz blurted eventually, coming out less like a blurt and more like a whisper, 'he asked me to marry him.'

At this Ferangiz looked up from her paper the shock apparent, her eyes widening through the long-sighted lenses of her spectacles. Even she had not expected things to move quite this fast. Her chest rose. Sudden. Then fell.

'And?'

Mehnaz looked down, unable to say it out loud.

There was a long pause.

'Please don't be a fool Mehnaz,' her voice stern and cold.

Mehnaz looked up into the grey eyes of her aunt, 'I love him, Izzy Aunty.'

Ferangiz lost her usual straight-backed composure, her hands at her forehead in vexation. 'You're too young Mehnaz for goodness sake! Is this the girl I've brought you up to be? You must first finish your studies and then you're free to do what you want.'

But you cannot bring a girl up to be her own person and then expect her not to be.

'But I can continue my studies in Delhi! I'll still be a paediatrician! You know I will! I'll still make you proud!'

'Let me make it very clear Mehnaz, if you go ahead and marry that boy you'll never make me proud.'

'Don't Izzy Aunty, don't do this. Don't punish me. You know how much I need your blessing.'

'I'm not punishing you Mehnaz, I'm protecting you. In this I cannot give you my blessing. If you marry him, you will not have it. Period. I refuse to endorse this nonsense even if your candy-headed mother does. I refuse to give you permission to ruin your life.'

'But Izzy Aunty! Don't you remember, don't you remember what it was like? Don't you remember how it was when you met Homi Uncle!'

The words were out of her mouth before she could stop them, even the kindest among us having the power to hurt when we are struck, though in truth it was more a plea, a desperate appeal, than a cruel dig.

Mehnaz was on her feet at once, overwrought. 'I'm so sorry, Izzy Aunty! I didn't mean to say that! I'm so sorry!'

Ferangiz did again what she knew how to do best. The fortress flew up and she placed a moat of imperious cold between herself and her niece.

'Unlike your Uncle Homi whom you never had the good fortune to meet, this man whom you have decided you are in love with is a chancer. For all his polished appearance there's not a decent bone in his body, I can tell you that now. I didn't want to say that to you, but you'll find out. You'll never have my support on this. If you won't listen you're on your own, Mehnaz. Well, you have your mother. That reminds me…'

At this Izzy Aunty took her red pen, and tearing a bit of the newspaper she scratched something on it, nib furious, handing it to Mehnaz.

'Give this to her.'

Mehnaz took it, hands shaking.

'Please, Izzy Aunty…'

But Ferangiz had picked up her newspaper. The drawbridge was up.

CHAPTER 15

Mehnaz stumbled across the yard in tears. This was not how it was supposed to be. She had tripped gaily through life, love swirling around her at each turn, and she had never, not really, had the rug pulled from under her feet. Even the death of her father, she, so young at the time – only just six years old – seemed not to have fully touched her, maybe because she was so cossetted and enwrapped by Izzy Aunty and her mother that his absence never left a lasting vacuum.

She lay on her bed and sobbed. Her mother found her there.

'Oh Mehnu darling, don't listen to her. It will all be ok!'

'It's not ma, it's not!' she wailed. 'I can't bear that she's angry with me, I need her blessing! I just don't know what to do!'

'She'll come around eventually Mehnaz, I'm sure. You have to do what you want; you can't live your life for your aunt. You have my blessing, you know that.'

Mehnaz nodded, trying her best to convey it counted as much, then remembering the paper Izzy Aunty had handed to her still scrunched up in her hand. She unscrunched it, opening it to iron out the creases before handing it to her mother, as she did so glancing at what Izzy Aunty had scratched in the now smudged ink.

'27 December 1998'

She frowned through her tears, a date, 10 years from now?

'Izzy Aunty gave me this to give you.'

Farida looked at it and Mehnaz thought she saw something like fear cross her mother's face.

'What is it, ma?'

'Just one of your aunt's games,' said her mother, scrunching it up again and throwing it rather forcefully into the old wire dustbin.

She stroked Mehnaz's hair.

'Manoj called by the way.'

And just like that a flush shot through her veins, everything inside her leaping. Mehnaz knew she had no choice. And there, just like that, it was done.

CHAPTER 16

Meanwhile back in Delhi, Manoj panted on top of Priti in the rooftop barsati – the little independent annex room at the top – that they used as a love nest whenever the coast was clear, or her husband was out of town. It was mid-afternoon. God, he thought, as he pumped, her legs wrapped tightly around his back, he needed this; rolling over and pulling her with him, Priti enthusiastically bouncing atop him despite the heat, then turning herself around to face the other way so he had a full view of her tight rising and falling rear. Oh, she was *good*! Priti had missed him while he'd been gone and Manoj was reaping the benefits as she attended to him magnificently, showing the Kama Sutra a thing or two and proving a couple of pages missing. As he came though, it was not hers, but the imagined image of Mehnaz's plump bucking rear, that had him come in a violent rush.

They lay there panting together, he dimly aware he hadn't yet told her he was getting married and that things would soon change. Oh well, he thought, absently tweaking her nipple and getting aroused once more, Priti ever ready and parting herself again for him, he'd tell her soon.

Part Five

MISS MISTRY

CHAPTER 1

In the flurry that necessarily accompanies approaching weddings, Mrs. Prabhakar was especially flurried, competing in this only with Farida, who having acquiesced to a Delhi ceremony for reasons of Ferangiz and finance in that order wanted to be involved as much as the boy's mother. The two discussed everything from the shade of the flowers to the length of the rice grains, over which the phone conversations between Delhi and Poona were long, circular and detailed. The two women having begun with a mutual complicity, both independently wanting their respective children to wed, found themselves at first in synch but later engaged in mini-power battles which Mehnaz patiently and occasionally Manoj less patiently had to mediate, not counting the skirmishes that fell to Bina to referee.

'I tell you,' Farida would complain to Bina, 'her taste is just so gaudy.' And in her other ear Mrs. Prabhakar would grumble, 'Every detail she wants to know about yah, and wants to bring her own cook to the wedding, I mean what is wrong with my cooks?!' At other times, Farida would say to Bina, 'I mean just how many people does she want to invite, it will look as if her family is big and our family is small, like we are just turning up for their parade.' In this she needn't have worried too much, as Manoj put his foot down when he caught sight of the guest list as long as

203

a sari, snipping it down ruthlessly despite his mother's cries and protests – Ma, it's a wedding not a coronation – this privately coming as something of a surprise to his mother. And so it went on. However, since the Prabhakars were largely footing the bill and the marriage was on their turf, Mrs. Prabhakar slipped a lot more past Farida than Farida knew, so when the big day arrived there were rather a lot of not altogether agreeable surprises. But arrive it did, and when all were gathered around the ceremonial fire to witness the young couple walk around it to fuse their union – at about or exactly 11.20 am on 23 November 1988, a date and time chosen at random as Manoj refused to have any pundits on the case – there was one person missing. Not apparent then to most of the guests, but to two women and one in particular – a young woman who walked around the fire behind her husband to be, her step a little sadder than the happy occasion warranted – it was very, very apparent indeed.

CHAPTER 2

Being left behind alone has a particular sort of silence, the clang of a gate or the slam of a door in an empty house, quite, quite different from an occupied one. Almost as if, we, our bodies, absorb the edges, softening and rounding it for each other and it falls less sharply.

When the marriage party left for Delhi, when the gate finally clanged after the many to-ing and fro-ings to the waiting taxis, the forgotten items ran back for, everything loaded up for the Nizamuddin Express – Mehnaz's trousseau and her college books, the family's suitcases packed with outfits for each ceremony, Hema's masalas and coconut oil – and they all finally bundled in, there were no excited shouts of goodbye, no exuberant waves, no blown kisses. No, when the gate clanged and the taxis pulled away their engines straining under the weight of the baggage, it was to silence. Nobody could be joyous, at least not within earshot. It was difficult for everyone, and very, very painful for one of the departing party in particular.

As the taxis were being saddled and just as everyone had started getting in, Mehnaz had made her way haltingly over to her aunt's verandah, having not done so since being shut out, though she had begun and faltered many times. There had been a Cold War at Balthazar House in the weeks after the proposal; Izzy Aunty having been civil to her and the family but that was all. Although the coldness had come from one side only, Mehnaz was bereft without her aunt's company and counsel. Knowing her aunt the way she did though, she also knew that at least for now there was nothing she could do. As she walked around the side of the house this early morning, she tried not to expect anything at all, knowing that offsetting disappointment would be the safest strategy, but try as she might, she couldn't not hope that her aunt would give her *something* – a tiny blessing, a word of warmth, any acknowledgement.

When she reached the verandah however, before she could even walk up the steps, Ferangiz spoke without looking up as if to stop her there.

'Goodbye, Mehnaz.'

Despite all her preparation Mehnaz reeled, the cold tone slamming into her like a swinging spiked hammer.

When time is run out and we're at our last gasp, on deathbeds, at airports, on long Poona driveways, we do things that we would ordinarily never do, say things we don't normally say, cross boundaries we wouldn't otherwise cross, all the things that matter that lie deep in our hearts but don't find their way into the everyday, spilling out in a tearful rush. Here was no different. We see Mehnaz running up the steps across the verandah, flinging her arms around her aunt – her aunt who stiffly denies embrace even with Mehnaz – crying, 'I love you so much Izzy Aunty,' then turning and running, running, running, running for the gate, her red dupatta flying in the crimson dawn, collapsing into the cab and the waiting arms of her mother. The cars set off, Mehnaz's sobbing the only sound within them as they wound down the lane, round the corner, into the city and away from home.

Ferangiz, sat on her verandah, very stiff, very straight and very still, the departing sounds reaching her ear like a receding echo until there were no more.

CHAPTER 3

In the 53 years that Ferangiz had spent in Balthazar ever since the day she was born, she had never actually been all alone in the house; her sister or the girls, and before that Anosh, and before that her mother, and before that her father, and seemingly permanently Hema, there had always been someone at home. Now only Raju was left, and, as for the first time in his employ he was not being ordered around by Hema, he took the opportunity to slope off with his broom and have a nap in one of the cool, shady outhouses, descending into a peaceful slumber of the kind he had not had in living memory. The rhinoceros was away and Raju could stray, and stray he did, wandering off into a somnambulous dreamland that was free of thundering orders and filled with a heavenly corridor of cottony cumulus clouds, atop which he wafted without a care.

So there was not even the dependable sound of him sweeping the yard to insulate Ferangiz as the silence descended over the house. And though she had spent much of her adult years wishing the family would pipe down or clear off, now that they had, in the way that they had, she did not know how to occupy the empty space they left behind.

For the third time in her life, Ferangiz found herself staring over the edge of a cliff and into the void. A void left by someone who had taken residence deep in her heart only to leave forever, suddenly and starkly, and she left behind again, her hull empty, a skeleton once more. Was this what life was? To have and to lose? To hold only for a short while? What design fault in the fabric of existence was this, that we must all at one time or another, and mostly over and over, have our innards ripped and torn apart by the departure of those we hold deepest and dearest.

A dark inky blue seeped through her.

In the end she could stand it no longer. She rose, walking round her verandah and into the main house. Wandering from room to empty room, loitering in the lounge her hand on the back of the blue and white rocking chair, her weight tilting it into motion, the steel bows grinding on the stone floor. Unoccupied space, unoccupied sound, it seems, lets old things, forgotten things, flood in, the stage no longer crowded by busyness and chatter. Her father on the sofa, his foot treadling the rocking chair like a sewing machine, while she held on, her feet not reaching the floor, saying 'more dada, more' when he stopped, pretending his foot had fallen off tucking it into the ankles of his trousers. She sat on the sofa. Then there was Mehnaz, maybe seven or eight years old, standing in front of her while she double knotted her tie, Mehnaz dancing from one foot to the other, the way she could never stand still; Izzy touching her affectionately on her nose as she scampered off. Mehnaz sprawled on her tummy on her verandah, scrawling untidily at her sums, 'look Izzy Aunty, look I've done them!' Mehnaz sailing past her on her new red bike, aged 9 or 10, 'look Izzy Aunty, look!' and crashing straight into the mango tree. Explaining to Mehnaz why she couldn't walk with her to school, why the other kids would be jealous and why in class she was not allowed to call her Izzy Aunty. 'In school you are all the same Mehnaz, but at home you are my little kaleja ok?' Mehnaz nodding, her face flushed with something that looked like pride.

There in the quiet of the great house memory sieved over memory, till her mind in an almost eerie way was filled with voices and shifting images, the dust taking form, genie-like, hearing her father's voice singing to her, 'hello Izzy, why hello Izzy,' and the evening seemed to whisper with the soft whinny of horses.

Dusk started to settle and through it came the whisk and husk of the broom. Raju must have woken up. Ferangiz realized vaguely that she hadn't eaten. Hema had prepared some simple meals for her, for while she was gone – dal and parathas, vegetables, some fish – packing it into little stainless-steel boxes in the fridge and putting most in the freezer. She took a box out now putting a little on a plate, sitting down at the head of the table, alone. But she had no appetite and rose a few minutes later to return it to the Kelvinator. Raju appeared in the kitchen doorway, his thin bowed legs forming a harp against the setting evening. Ferangiz asked him to lock up for the night as she took herself back to her verandah and then to her room, the silence now enveloping, thick and black as the approaching dark.

CHAPTER 4

She went to school, she taught the children, she came home, she tutored the children. Either side of that she simply sat still on her verandah , her chair now angled away from the gate. At night she continued her room-to-room wandering; her insides re-configuring, adjusting, adapting, steeling, getting ready for the family's return, the return she dreaded, the return without her Mehnaz. Every night she sat at the dining table at its head as usual, the hurt and fury if it had diminished over the course of the day, returning at each solo meal. It was less that she had been 'disobeyed' this was not how Ferangiz saw it. For all her authority she was not entirely an autocrat. It was simply that she knew she was right. Mehnaz was going to ruin her life and her stupid mother not only couldn't see it but had *arranged* it and if that was not enough had done so far away from them in Delhi, Ferangiz banging her fist involuntarily on the table in anger and frustration startling Raju who was waiting outside to lock up. With each passing day her iron fist tightened a little more, till by the time the family was almost due to return from Delhi, Ferangiz was hardened into a new resolve. She was right. Time would tell them of course – she knew that – but in the meantime she was going to prove it; she was going to show everyone and especially that foolish, noodle-brained Farida, just *how* right she was.

CHAPTER 5

When Farida and the family returned from Delhi, they were greeted by an unusual sight. Instead of Ferangiz sitting alone on the verandah as she always was at this time of day once her students had left, another chair had been placed next to her – it looked like it was one from the lounge. In it was sat a middle-aged gentleman, rather slender and bookish, with thick glasses and lightly greying hair, leaning forward nodding fervently at whatever Ferangiz was saying. They were both looking at a largish sheet of paper laid out on the small table between them, Ferangiz's pen pointing out this, then that, as she periodically looked up at him, neither turning once towards the opening gate.

The family exchanged a shocked glance, each of their faces bearing an increasing scale of scandalised alarm, Farida more toward the right end of the scale, Almaz's eyes bulging around the middle and even Hema's goitre on full alert. Who was this gentleman? Surely not a beau?!

They all knew never to interrupt her – their awkwardness about Delhi notwithstanding – so they had to wait till dinner when Ferangiz joined them, though she simply ate her food exchanging minimal pleasantries and then got up and left the table not enquiring about Delhi or their journey and certainly not about the wedding, leaving no room equally for counter enquiry. At the end of the meal then they were all none the wiser about the visitor, though perfectly clear that the line that had been drawn before Mehnaz's wedding was no longer in the sand but cemented in.

A few days later, the bookish gentleman was once again back on Ferangiz's verandah, arriving after the tuition pupils had left in the early evening, this time accompanied by two younger men in their thirties – one portly, wearing short sleeves, high waisted trousers and a furrowed expression and the other equally furrowed though not quite as high-waisted, his tummy barrelling over the tops of his trousers and resting a fair furlong forward on to his solid, expansive thighs. Sweat beaded on both men's faces and laked under their armpits as they all clustered around the little table on the verandah – two more chairs having been brought from the lounge – listening intently to what Ferangiz was saying, both nodding, the lower-waisted one taking notes, the higher-waisted leaning over to double check he'd done so correctly.

None of the family were privy to what was going on and none of them, not even Almaz, had the temerity to dare ask. Consternation was at a high. What was Ferangiz Aunty up to? Well, let's see…if we were to fly a little closer, perhaps not calling on Kalina she being busy with larger themes, but appropriating a sparrow nesting atop one of the old pillars – one would have heard the following murmured in hushed tones:

'So, Jupiter has a shadow over your tenth house, which means at this time in your business you must be careful. The last time this happened was nine years ago, you had something happen then?'

'9 years ago? Oh Rama! Yes, ma'am that was when our factory was destroyed in the fire! Oh my God!'

'No, don't panic,' Ferangiz's voice was authoritative and calm. 'It will not be like that this time and whatever happens you will recover quickly. But be careful of the deals you make and with whom; double check and triple check any offers of partnership. It will turn out well, but only if you have your wits about you. Do your background checks, do your diligence and you could possibly see the results of Jupiter's move to the wealth section of your chart as soon as May.'

At this the two brothers beamed, relaxing a little in their chairs, their tummies flopping with relief one inside his trousers and the other's over the top, 'Thank you Mistry ma'am, thank you'.

No one in the house knew who these men were but we have met one of them before – the slender, greying, bookish one we may recognize as Mr. Joshi from the bookshop. Dear Mr. Joshi who had been sourcing astrology books for Ferangiz for years now, sometimes asking her as he wrapped them for her in brown paper, half joking, half earnest, for who amongst us is not curious about our own fate, 'Miss Mistry you must be an expert now, when will you read my stars?'

'It's just a personal interest, Mr Joshi,' having finally admitted the books were for indeed her. 'Now about that volume you were telling me about last time – the Raphael's Ephemeris – did you have any luck with that one?'

'It should be in next time, about 4 weeks they said, but they are being very slow!'

And despite her steadfast response, the same every time, it's just a personal interest Mr Joshi, every so often he would ask her again.

Well, it seems in life persistence pays or certainly asking for what you want does, as much as sometimes it doesn't. But on this fateful day – the 30th of November 1988 – a day like any other when it began, Mr Joshi

214

jokingly asked Ferangiz again whether she would read his stars and she looked straight at him and said 'Ok, Mr Joshi, I will. Tell me, when is your birth date?'

'My goodness, Miss Mistry are you serious?'

'Yes. Why don't you come to the house day after tomorrow in the evening at 5.30 pm. Write down your birth date for me now, do you know your exact birth time?'

'I can get it'.

'Send it to me ahead'

"Yes ma'am, I'll send the peon.' Mr Joshi looked a little anxious, despite his cajoling he'd never really expected her to say yes. Now, perfectly content as he was with his life, with his family and his little bookshop, the prospect of looking into his future made him nervous, afraid of what he might find. After all these years of gentle pestering he didn't feel he could now backpedal, so after going home and asking his wife to look up his birth certificate, he duly sent his peon Jagesh on his rickety bike with a handwritten note on which was scribbled the exact date and time of his arrival into this world, turning up at the appointed time at Balthazar Drive to a cup of very good tea and an awaiting chair on a verandah of an otherwise seemingly empty house.

Miss Mistry sat in the chair opposite him opening out a sheet of paper that had arcs and angles and various crosses, notes and marks, saying to him without further ado, getting straight down to business examining the chart as she did so, 'Mr. Joshi you have had a peaceful life, a good life, an intellectual life. You are a contented man.' Mr. Joshi smiled with relief. She continued. 'Financially you are stable, adequate, no great riches, nor it seems do you long for them but stable all the same.' Mr Joshi beamed. 'Healthwise everything is fine, the odd blip here and there but nothing to worry about?' He nodded happily, 'Yes Miss Mistry, my diabetes is under control with medication.'

Just at that moment the gate of Balthazar Drive opened and there was a bit of a commotion as people got out and suitcases got unloaded and doors were slammed and drivers were paid, but Miss Ferangiz Mistry did not look up, so other than a cursory glance neither did he, because also just at that moment Miss Mistry said, 'You have a daughter Mr. Joshi?' He nodded.

'I am seeing something touching your chart from her side. Is all well with her, with her marriage?'

'Why Miss Mistry, what can you see!' he cried, 'I think everything is fine?'

At this Ferangiz looked up and very kindly but seriously said to him, 'I think you should check on her Mr Joshi. Keep an eye. Ask her discretely if things are ok. She may be needing your help or even to come home for a while. Don't worry all will be ok, just check on her.'

Mr Joshi trying not to sound too concerned duly did. His daughter hearing him ask quite so specifically about her wellbeing and wondering how on earth he knew, started weeping into the phone, 'Papa, it's nothing papa.' And the humble bookseller who wouldn't harm a fly got the train that very day and travelled to Bombay, arriving at midday, knocking on her door, she cowering behind it covering her face that was black and blue and he bundling her out of the house and straight into an autorickshaw and to the bus station out of the domestic hell she had been living in, too scared to leave or say.

Such is the debt we owe those who save our lives or even more the lives of those we love, that we never forget it, holding them ever in highest regard or eternal devotion. Such was Mr. Joshi's gratitude, that to him Miss Mistry was a heaven-sent angel. A heaven-sent angel who had been visiting his store for all of these years, for whom he had sourced the rarest of books filled with the rarest of knowledge, who had offered to tell his fortune at the very moment when it was needed – even a month before being too early and even a day later who knows, God forbid, maybe being too late – all for the divine purpose of ultimately saving the creature in the world that he loved the most.

To say that he sung Ferangiz's praises was an understatement; it was a devotional hymn, his wife and daughter joining in the grateful refrain. As a result, it wasn't long before Mr Joshi's nephews asked if

Miss Mistry would be able to see them too. They were in the middle of nervously signing a partnership deal to save their ailing business, so Mr Joshi asked on their behalf, 'Would you mind ma'am seeing my nephews also?' Ferangiz said yes, they too taking a pew on her verandah to hear what the stars could tell. On her advice – or more accurately warning – after some investigation they reneged on the deal, the pair signing instead with a smaller concern, this proving lucrative beyond their dreams, and by May of that year, exactly as she predicted, once again turning a profit and the rupees rolling in.

That took the count of eternal gratitude from five people directly to easily fifty or more by association, for when our fortunes turn so do the fortunes of those around us. The snowball became an avalanche, or since we are on the hot plains of India without a snowflake in sight, let's say the loo wind gathered and began to blow with news of the teacher who could tell the future.

Word soon spread of the Parsi astrologer with a sensitivity of interpretation and an accuracy of reading that only comes along once in a very long while so as to become legendary; the nephews bringing cousins and the cousins bringing aunties and the aunties bringing uncles, nieces, nephews, mamajis and dadajis, until Mr. Joshi volunteered to become her private secretary, offering his services pro bono and handling the bookings and requests, first come first served, no favouritism, no string pulling or connections, 'I don't care whether you are a Birla or a Gandhi or a Nehru,' he would say, 'you will have to wait,' being as he was a democratic and upstanding man himself and sensing that Miss Mistry hated any sort of favouritism.

Her appointments forward-booked into the next month and the next, the ringing phone and clamouring requests starting to interrupt the effective running of his bookshop, Mr Joshi's devotion such that Miss Mistry came first, she was paramount, his wife and daughter and even the nephews' wives coming into help run the store, all the while he taking it upon himself to make sure Miss Mistry's commitments allowed for enough rest. 'You must not work so hard ma'am,' he'd frown worriedly as Ferangiz sat down with the eager and the anxious for their readings after a long day of teaching and tuitions, 'I'll not take any appointments for you for two weeks, take some rest ma'am.' But she would shake her head, 'No Mr. Joshi, I live for my work.' Not forgetting between us that Ferangiz was a woman of singular purpose. And also privately that she had a point to prove.

And so, much to Farida's chagrin, the queue grew, snaking down the lane and through the years, the entire nation it seemed asking, waiting, coming from far and near, patiently attendant or urgently clamouring for her sister – the gifted astrologer who was never wrong.

Part Six

MANOJ

CHAPTER 1

Meanwhile in the sprawling capital city far up in the north, a city of grand enclaves and esplanades, of filthy chawls and spider lanes, of trucks and ring roads, forts and tombs, of the haves and will-never-haves, in this city that sat supreme atop India, the bindu in her forehead, here in one of its leafy colonies the lives of Mehnaz and Manoj spooled out like a rolling carpet on to which they stepped and their lives together began.

Their lives together began in the carnal culmination of the chemical reaction that had ignited not so long ago when the gates had clanged and her breasts had collided with his chest, setting off a fission of desire that exploded when finally the wedding rites were over, the congratulations received, the wishes well-wished. When finally they got into the white Mercedes that despite his orders his mother had gotten covered in marigolds and carnations – Manoj burning slightly redder than the blossoms with embarrassment and annoyance, this was going to do nothing for his reputation of a man of understated class, grateful nonetheless that it wasn't a carriage led by horses and elephants, he wouldn't have put it past her – and drove off to the Leela Palace hotel for the night. Waving to the guests as the garlanded car pulled away, his hands immediately drew her close. His arms wrapped around her waist finding the bare bit just above the tuck line of her sari, moving upwards tantalizingly under the pallu, just grazing the weighty under-curve of her breasts, ignoring the presence of the driver in the front seat and his studiously centred eyebrows. When they got to the hotel room they did not go through a tender ritual of sweet nothings, they didn't dance to soft music, they didn't hold hands and look out over the twinkling city or admire the rose petals beautifully strewn over their nuptial bed. The hotel room door closed behind them and he pulled her towards him, his kurta already making an admirable silk tent, kissing her deep and long as he started to unwind her sari saying 'I wanted to do this at the gate the first time I saw you,' turning her around and around, swivelling her slowly from her hips, his hands tracing her as she turned until the last of the sari fell to the floor, cascades of red and gold around her pretty stilettoed feet, as she stood in her silk blouse and petticoat, her lovely plump curves there for him to see. And then the moment that he had been waiting for – the first moment – and the moment that she had been waiting for and afraid of too – the first time. He drew her in again, his hands undoing her blouse slowly, then her bra, her breasts spilling out, so naked, into his gasping hands, her sari petticoat untied and falling to the floor, her panties coming off and him kneeling before her, his eyes and tongue finding her, she dying of shock and delight as she discovered her body's own generosity and pleasure, then him revealed, a little alarming, as her hands found him for the first time, its curious hardness and vulnerability and seeming life of its own, and then he was upon her and the carnal adventure that would mark the early years of their marriage began.

He could never put his finger on it…that effect she had on him. He felt like a bee burrowing into a rose of such fragrant sweetness, cushioned in such creamy plumpness, that he was lost in a carnal honeysuckled crib. For her, his demand, his surety, how was he so experienced she sometimes wondered, his possession of and delight in her body making her flower even more, sweet nectar, sweet nectar, sweet nectar. They fucked. A lot. Morning, evening, night. In the kitchen, on the bathroom floor, against the wall, sometimes in the bedroom, sometimes the bed, the only thing inhibiting them being the arrival of the cook in the morning, with the possibility of being discovered in flagrante thrilling Manoj and horrifying Mehnaz.

It made concentrating on her college work difficult. She'd be knee deep in scientific journals – having enrolled to finish her medical degree in Delhi – only to find that she had been staring at the paper on complications with tropical diseases in children without registering any of the significant facts, her knickers permanently damp, not just down to the sizzling heat either. Manoj did not make it any easier. He would come home from work in the late evening to find her sat at the dining table surrounded by piles of books, her curly hair frizzing in all directions and he would set down his briefcase, take off his tie and suckle her breasts while she read. 'Manoj!' she would cry, 'I have to concentrate! I'm going to fail if I don't!' But then she would turn herself towards him and he would part her willing legs and burrow his head between them. It always felt so pure with her he thought, unbuttoning his trousers, lowering her on to the floor and penetrating her soft, willing flesh; the pages of the Atlas of Paediatric Infectious Diseases fluttering in the breeze of the ceiling fan.

She enjoyed his devouring of her, discovering an appetite she hadn't known she had, happy to be endlessly lapped at as he explored every part of her. But she didn't really enjoy the parties. Manoj's career was flying high like the Supreme Court flag, even higher since his win in Poona, that trip having proved to be a fate-turning one in more ways than one and considerably upping the quality of his bacon. Invitation followed invitation. 'Manoj, I have to study, can't you go without me!' Mehnaz would protest, but Manoj wouldn't hear of it, Mehnaz was part of his package, his red-carpet consort. 'It'll be fun, baby,' he would say and even though Mehnaz found it anything but fun – being a natural born homebird who loved nothing more than to curl up otter-like and laugh and play, eat and snooze – not to mention the never-decreasing pile of books she had to get through. But for him she would don sari after sari, her curly hair would go up in a wanton bun, she would string on the pearls or the diamonds – subtle mind, not ostentatious, oh how

Manoj approved – slip on her stiletto heels and trip out with him and into another tinkling Delhi mansion. Sometimes she had dark rings under her eyes from having stayed up late and got up early, her eyes straining at weighty indexed volume after weighty indexed cross-referenced volume night after night and Manoj would comment on her looking tired although more – was she imagining that – with criticism than concern. He would look across the room at her every now again, people curling around her because with Mehnaz people just did, and he would puff up with what she thought was pride in her and flush happily behind her tired young eyes as she silently worried beneath the chatter how she would ever catch up with her work fretting that she was going to flunk it.

But no niece of Ferangiz would fail and despite the gruelling syllabus of her degree sandwiched between Manoj's attentions, the social demands of being a successful lawyer's wife and having to manage a home, Mehnaz managed to wrestle the flagellates; rare bacteria; dreaded viruses; the gastrointestinal, respiratory, cardiovascular, haematological, nervous, endocrine and genetic disorders; together with their symptoms, treatments, indications, contra-indications and all their Latin names into her memory and understanding, managing a pretty respectable mark even if not quite as high as her glittering Poona standards, still respectable enough in the top 10%. See Izzy Aunty, see! I said I'd do it, she mentally said to her aunt, I'll never let you down. And in all of this demand and busyness, she would buy an inland aerogramme, her untidy scrawl covering the blue paper, *Dearest Izzy Aunty* she would write, as Izzy Aunty never came to the phone when she called home which she did every week, *Dearest Izzy Aunty, I just got my exam results today. I think you'll be proud of me*, filling the limited space with her marks and thoughts on what went well and what she could have done better just as she would have if she was sat on Izzy Aunty's verandah, mentioning Manoj in a small way so as not to be insensitive nor falsely deny his existence, and always signing it with *I miss you, Your Mehnaz*. Which she did, terribly, terribly.

Her Izzy Aunty never replied.

It's a long road to becoming a paediatrician and year of study, followed year of study, till after four years – having already done a year in Poona – Mehnaz was ready for the three years required in clinical practice before she could carry the letters M.D after her name. It had not been easy even getting this far, which was only two-thirds of the way there, and sometimes the only thing that kept her going with it was that somewhere in her heart she carried an image, an image that she had had as long as she could remember almost as if she had been born with it imprinted on her DNA – an image of a small thin child with a wheezing bony chest on whom she laid a stethoscope warmed between her hands, and of leaning into listen

228

so that she could hear what her little body was saying it needed to heal – and when the nights got too long, when her head felt she could no longer retain a single useful or useless fact, when she sat down to her books after returning from another function that Manoj had needed her to attend, when her eyelids would droop heavy with lead and all her body wanted to do was sleep, she would hold that image and it would hold her and she would keep going.

And every month she wrote to Izzy Aunty, *Dearest Izzy Aunty*, she'd write, *I'm finding that pound for pound babies are actually stronger than oxen. Izzy Aunty, I treated three little children today. Izzy Aunty, I had a glimpse of what it would be like when I have my own clinic. Izzy Aunty, how will I ever remember this for the exam. Izzy Aunty I came first, Izzy Aunty I came first, Izzy Aunty I came first.*

Izzy Aunty never replied.

CHAPTER 2

With all the demands on her, she couldn't visit home. Poona or rather Balthazar was still home, she not yet having crossed the threshold to the point when suddenly the new place we move to, without warning after years of it not being, suddenly becomes home. She missed it. Though her mother and sometimes the girls visited her, in those four years of gruelling medical study she only made it back once – for Almaz's sixteenth birthday. Mehnaz was so excited she couldn't sleep for weeks before. It seemed to rile Manoj. She was only going for three days, Manoj wanted her back for the annual conference dinner plus she had an exam the following week, but she wasn't going to miss Almaz's big day for anything. Almaz had been on the phone every two minutes despite her mother's protests in the background, 'Almaz do you have any idea how much it costs to call Delhi!' Almaz wanting to tell her sister who was coming, what she was wearing, what the menu was, including giving Mehnaz a menu list of options of all her desired presents.

Mehnaz flew down to Poona and they were all there at the airport waiting for her – well, almost all – her mother, Almaz and Shanaz in an excited row. They chattered together all at once, a flock of animated parrots with a silent crane humming contentedly in their midst, Shanaz having become tall and slender with her aunt's grey eyes. So it was a happy gaggle that piled into the taxi, clambering atop each other not able to get close enough, tumbling out again at Balthazar. Almaz pushed open the gates, taking the lead in possession and pride that Mehnaz was home for *her* and they all walked through, their chatter quieting automatically. Mehnaz heard the familiar creak and squeak of the old hinges, feeling the cool familiar shade of the orchard glide over her, as Auto ran up to greet them thwacking her with his bottom. Hema was waiting, a big beam across her formidable face – Hema only beamed when complimented on her food, so this was significant – standing on the porch to welcome her home.

Mehnaz's eyes went straight over to the verandah. There, sat with her back turned away from the gate was Izzy Aunty… but wait, not alone. There were two lounge chairs arranged around the low table in which were sat a youngish couple. Mehnaz's throat caught. She had been replaced!

'Who are they?' she asked her mother as they walked up to the porch.

'Oh, your aunt is doing astrology now. There's always someone coming to see her,' Farida said a little too offhandedly.

'Astrology?!'

Nobody ever mentioned Izzy Aunty to her, through a sensitivity or an avoidance one is never quite sure, everyone knowing how bereft Mehnaz had been at her aunt's distancing and especially her absence at her wedding. Even when she asked, which she always did when she phoned home, 'How is Izzy Aunty?' she got the usual 'She's fine, busy with her work.' So to say she was a little taken aback at both this scene and the news of astrology, was a little bit like the civilizations of yesteryear might have felt when being told that the earth was not a flat table top carried upon the back of a turtle, but was in fact an azure and emerald ball hurtling around a golden sun with all of us pinned to it by gravity.

As much as her heart had plummeted on seeing her aunt deep in conversation with the couple on their verandah, her jaw now dropped. Her aunt, her academic, scientific, empirical aunt was now an astrologer?!

'What are you talking about ma?!'

'She decided to study it and now has become an expert apparently. There're always people coming to see her,' her tone saying more about the frosty relationship between herself and her sister than any amount of denial or explanation.

'Since when?! When did this start? Why did no one tell me?'

'What am I supposed to say Mehnu? She hardly talks to us anymore. Hello, bye, has dinner that's it.'

Then looking over at her daughter who was looking over at the verandah, a crooked expression on her face, she took her hand, 'Don't expect anything while you're here Mehnu, you'll only get hurt...'

Although Farida wasn't known for sage advice, this proved sage advice indeed as Ferangiz did not join the table for dinner even once while Mehnaz was there. Suddenly it seemed she had a pressing imperative to see not one punter wanting their future told, but three in a row leaving no gaps in between, having Hema send her a small plate of food at 8.30 pm and promptly retiring for the night. Leaving for school early, surrounded by tuition students in the afternoon and then attending to the waiting fortune seekers after, left no vacant interval where Mehnaz could approach – she not having to be a fully qualified doctor to work out that this was intentional.

She had not expected much from Izzy Aunty; her unanswered letters signal enough that her aunt had not yet found it in her heart to embrace her. But she certainly had not expected to not even get a single word of greeting. It hurt her terribly. And though she was cheerful with the others and was the life and soul of her little sister's birthday party – baking her an enormous chocolate cake in the shape of the phone that Almaz was permanently attached to and decorating it in pink fondant icing, pink still being Almaz's absolute favourite colour, showering her with not one but *all* the presents that had been on Almaz's list – to say that underneath it all her heart was heavy would be the second major understatement of this particular visit.

Did this behaviour of Izzy Aunty contribute to the fact that over the years to come Mehnaz would not visit home at all? Almost certainly. Did this mean she did not miss it deeply? We know the answer to that. She could not bear to come home to this reception, initially asking Manoj, and then once she was earning well enough herself, booking air tickets for her mother and sisters to visit her more often in Delhi.

But she still wrote her. Not every month as she had done before, but at least three or so times a year, even

Mehnaz's devotion unable to withstand the stonewall of returning silence, and she never missed a birthday or Parsi New Year – of which, confusingly for all bewildered bystanders they are two a year.

Manoj never understood. 'Why are you writing to her yah,' he would say when he saw her sometimes sitting on the balcony penning away, occasionally looking upset. 'I don't know why you bother running after her like this.' And he would come up behind her and cup her breasts and kiss her neck, when what Mehnaz really needed was for him just to be with her and maybe stroke her hair.

'Not now, Manoj!' she would say. 'C'mon baby,' he persisted. And on these occasions and only on these occasions Mehnaz would get up and walk off, sometimes finding herself sobbing uncontrollably on their bed, uncertain whether she was upset about Izzy Aunty or was missing home or was just exhausted from the relentless study or whether, though she didn't like to think this thought, it was Manoj's pawing insensitivity and lack of concern. Manoj oblivious and annoyed fixed himself a whisky, sat out on the balcony looking over his city and wondered whether he should call Priti.

Wait, did we not mention Priti? That the barsati visits on the occasional afternoon continued? Oh! Well, they did. Doubtless there had been a lull in the very early days. Manoj was too besotted with Mehnaz to give Priti much thought, Priti's practiced ministrations and

234

athletic manoeuvrings even seeming to him repulsive and whorish in comparison to the rose who lay in his marital bed. No, initially in those first months, Manoj's head was buried between one pair of legs and one pair of legs only and those were the plump rosy thighs of Mrs Mehnaz Prabhakar. His head, his hands, his tongue, his feet, his ever-ready cock found her out, nesting, nestling, fingering, licking, burrowing, seeking, fucking; dying a different sort of ecstatic death when her mouth found him, and in all of that atomic pleasure Priti was completely forgotten. It would be exaggerating to say that she even crossed his mind once. Priti had found herself unceremoniously dumped, though Manoj had never said as much, he had simply disappeared off the scene and that was pretty much that.

But Priti's husband was away a lot and despite his well-stacked bank account, his pot belly, bald head and skinny legs not to mention strictly functional copulation did not exactly light her fire and she found herself both horny and bereft at Manoj's abrupt disappearance. She would call his office occasionally but his secretary, yes, he had a secretary now, would never put her through saying Manoj was in Lucknow on a case, in Calcutta on a case, in Bombay on a case, but Priti no shrinking violet herself made sure that he would get the message. 'Tell him Mrs. Kapoor from P M Enterprises called, it is important,' She duly did but Manoj dismissed the message without a second thought. At some point though, it's hard to know exactly when, maybe it was when Mehnaz was studying really hard and was tired all the time – though that feels more like a cliched excuse than the truth – or maybe it was that too much of a good thing eventually gets boring, or perhaps it was that variety was the spice of his life and who doesn't like a little bit of illicit sex and whorishness every now and again. Or perhaps it was none of those things. Maybe it was simply that one afternoon after Manoj had won a particularly prominent case, his adrenalin pumping from the victory, on a high and seeking release found himself thinking of Priti. It was a hot afternoon, the kind of afternoon that reminded him of sweating underneath her in the barsati, so before he got in the car to be driven back to the office his hand reached for the just-arrived mobile phone that was one of the privileged perks of his job and his fingers tapped the well-remembered number, Priti answering and Manoj saying, 'Hey baby, I've missed you, are you around?' And Priti, despite her hurt pride, at the sound of his voice felt that familiar rush between her legs, said 'If you come now, Suresh won't be back for another two, three hours,' she going up to the barsati that had an independent entrance from the rest of the house, taking off all her clothes and positioning herself rump up, presenting for Manoj's arrival. His footsteps on the stairs had her writhe in anticipation, so when Manoj walked into the room she was fuck-ready. He

236

was in her in seconds – he didn't have long – and they were done all too soon, wiping his dick dry and kissing her fully on the lips before rushing back to the office and then home, his interlude with Priti leaving him even more turned on than usual and taking Mehnaz straight off to the bedroom floor as soon as he walked through the door.

This was just the sort of no-frills-all-thrills arrangement that suited him down to the ground and it was all too easy once the door had re-opened to welcome back his old ways. Over the years he had gathered convenient girls in most towns. Priti being in Delhi was his most constant, and if he was truthful he had more of a soft spot for her than he would care to admit, particularly as he preferred to think of Mehnaz as his type. Even so, in Bombay there was the young catholic Anglo Indian trainee lawyer Cecilia, who showed a cavalier and catholic disregard for contraception and allowed Manoj to have her entirely unsheathed in his hotel bedroom and sometimes in his office after hours. In Calcutta, there were the legendary Bengali girls, as honeyed and creamy as their Mishti Doi and Rupa, though he paid her – he didn't want too many complications and secretly enjoyed the transactional power it gave him – kept him ungainfully occupied. Let's stop there lest this turn into an inland sailor story. We get the picture.

All of this as we have already said, did not diminish his desire for Mehnaz, it fuelled it, the erotic images he carried from his buccaneering adventures raising the charge. Mehnaz was mostly delighted by his insatiable wanting of her and when he came home to her the two would be very quickly at it again. Sooner or later the inevitable happened and just as Mehnaz began her last year in clinician practice before her full qualification, his scattered sperm made it through and the young paediatrician started her first job, rather eponymously in the family way.

CHAPTER 3

She shone with happiness. The cook at home fed her almonds soaked overnight. Manoj's mother fussed around her, proud that her son had spawned an imminent young calf. Keen to ensure that Mehnaz delivered it perfectly, she would check on her working hours, lecture her on nutrition and bring over pastes of turmeric and cream to rub into her swelling tummy and breasts. 'No man likes a stretch-marked woman, Mehnaz,' she would say, and Mehnaz would smile graciously and thank her although she had no intentions of lathering herself in dairy products washing herself as usual with clear Pears soap as she sang happily in the shower. The staff in the clinic fussed over her too. It hadn't taken long for them to decide that they wanted her for keeps and they would make her stop for lunch – which was a feat – reducing her long student hours so that she didn't work too late, and Mehnaz was soon not just a little grateful for that and happily accepted. Maybe it was also this, that she knew how to graciously receive, that made everyone love her so much, she knowing instinctively that it was part of love as much as giving was, making everyone feel loved in the bargain.

Her body burgeoned quickly, and Manoj was even more amorous than usual, nestling his head between her ballooning breasts and sucking on her spreading nipples, enjoying the enlarging lotus between her legs, it arousing him so much that he wanted more and more of it and Mehnaz would happily admonish him and say 'No Manoj, not in front of the children!' But when she threw up into the bucket in the bathroom in those first months, he would walk out of the bedroom on to the lounge balcony as far away as possible from the retching sounds, Mehnaz's head too deep in the bucket or toilet bowl to be able to see the look of revulsion on his face.

She worked all the way up to eight and a half months, propelled by the drive to qualify; she only had two months to go, and she was impatient for it. That impatience was also driven by another desire – wanting to say, 'look Izzy Aunty, look, I did it!' not in a told-you-so way, but in a way that said, will you believe me now, will you forgive me now, will you talk to me now?

But nature has no cause with our own timetables and first before any letters in the shape of M.D could be acquired or any duplicate certificates could be sent to imperious aunts, first another little girl with a mop of curly hair and her mother's disposition had to be born and born she was, Mehnaz bringing the nursing home down with unspeakable profanities and full-throated yells, as a little girl who they would name Diya finally shot out jubilantly into the world.

Mehnaz held her like a proud lioness for Manoj who walked through the door about or exactly two hours after it was all over having been caught up at work on a complicated case, he said. Manoj took the baby from her visibly puffing up with pride, his stride turned into a strut as he walked around the hospital room with her, his virility proved, his plumage on proud display. The young Mughal had a daughter, his perfect little Noor Jahan was here. Then he noticed the large ink-stain-shaped birthmark on Diya's forearm.

CHAPTER 4

Farida came to Delhi to look after the nursing Mehnaz. 'Ma!' Mehnaz cried happily when her mother came through the door, having been picked up at the airport by the driver, Manoj being at work and Mehnaz not wanting to leave the house with the infant

240

Diya yet. There are times in life when only mothers will do and this was one of them, Mehnaz not realizing quite how much she needed her until she sat next to her, one hand on Mehnaz's arm the other on the little baby's chin gently tilting Diya's face and saying, 'How pretty she is Mehnu,' looking at Mehnaz, beaming, then after some chatter taking her from her so Mehnaz could sleep.

Manoj came home late she noticed but always went to see the little girl sleeping in her cot in their bedroom, although one night she heard the couple arguing, Manoj saying he couldn't sleep and Mehnaz saying the baby had to be with them, Diya was not going to be put into a separate room. Mehnaz and the baby did indeed later decamp together to another bedroom so that Manoj could have an undisturbed sleep, and they would not be the first family to do so, thought Farida. Other than this however – the normal complaints of a working family with a newborn – Farida's observations judged the marriage a happy one. Perhaps we look for what we want to see, and that is the report she took back to the Balthazar dining table, broadcast within earshot of Ferangiz though not directly to her as the sisters didn't really speak to each other anymore.

Farida stayed on in Delhi until Mehnaz finally qualified, staying with them for a good part of that year so that after three months of nursing Diya, Mehnaz could return to the clinic for the morning session to finish what she had set out to do. It wasn't easy, and it was certainly not easy to leave Diya even for those few hours, but she knew she had to make the most of her mother being with her. Manoj didn't want Farida staying indefinitely; he hadn't said as much but his not-so-occasional irritation at the dining table, his sarcastically arched eyebrows at something her mother said or his longer than usual days in the office made Mehnaz feel that way. On top of this, his mother naturally wanted to help – and instruct – with the baby too and even with Mehnaz's diplomatic skills it wasn't always easy to manage the two women, and she didn't want Diya being the rope in a granny tug of war. So she nursed her baby and she did the morning clinic and she cajoled the two grandmothers and she mollified her husband, and occasionally she too slept.

In all of that, the letters finally came.

Mehnaz Prabhakar - M.D

CHAPTER 5

Farida returned to Poona with the duplicate certificates clutching them as proudly as if they were her very own, as if it were she herself who had slogged through the night for six long years. Mehnaz was going to post the large thin envelope with the certificate together with a picture of herself and Diya, but her mother said 'Don't' be silly Mehnaz, I'll take them with me when I go.' It had been her battle too and Farida wanted to show Ferangiz this certificate as much as Mehnaz did, she wanted to show Ferangiz the photographs of Diya as proudly as Mehnaz wanted to, except she also wanted to say 'See, you don't know everything, see you aren't always right!' But that wasn't all. She needed them for herself. She needed to clutch this document, this happy portrait of her daughter and baby to her breast, as proof that it had all been worth it, that the terrible chasm that Mehnaz's departure had left in their lives, the empty void that she had not fully anticipated was thus vindicated. So intent had she been on her freeing her daughter from the family curse, that she had simply not foreseen just how much it would fracture their lives and the life of Balthazar, nor the stillness her departure would leave. She hadn't been prepared for the loss of the everyday, of the nearness of her, and she needed to clutch these letters as her own certificate, as her own stamp that would say 'It was worth it.' And even as she flew back to Poona after a tearful airport farewell, kissing baby Diya and then hugging, hugging, hugging her Mehnaz, and even as the air hostess – that's what they were still called then – helped her with her seat belt, adjusting the strap and showing her how the buckle worked saying, 'Let me put that envelope in the over-head locker for you ma'am,' Farida shook her head and clutching onto it said, 'No, I need to keep it with me,' clutching it as the airplane taxied and took off, clutching it as she left her daughter once more on the hot plains of Delhi, clutching it all the way to Poona, holding on to it as the airport porter collected her bags and hailed her a taxi home.

And as she did, she couldn't help noticing how the thin, flat, brown envelope that contained all the exoneration she needed, that she had done the right thing, she had done the right thing, she had done the right thing, was no substitute, no substitute at all for the dimpled, warm shape and dappled sound of her daughter.

CHAPTER 6

In the interior of Ferangiz's quarters darkened by the aged, foggy panes that were once clear – not unlike her eyes that now needed thick soda glasses – darkened too by the mango trees that draped around her verandah shading it pleasantly but blocking the light, darkened by the old-fashioned lighting that could only illuminate isolated corners with a weak yellow glow, the surrounding damp blackness too pervasive for a single bulb to fight against, in this darkened interior was an old, very old, steel Godrej cupboard, referred to as the almirah.

In this almirah, with its creaking steel shelves slotted into place many years ago never to move again, were Ferangiz's spare possessions. A few handloom saris, starched and ironed by the dhobi so they could almost stand up unaided, hung crisply on thin, old, metal hangers. The matching blouses thread-worn, modest-sleeved, high-necked, lay folded one atop the other, neat and perfectly in line. A few sari petticoats, mostly old-white, lay ironed beside them.

Also inside the almirah, securely welded in above the shelves, was the necessary inner sanctum of every Godrej cupboard – an independently lockable wall-to-wall metal safe. Elsewhere in all of India, if you were to open the safes of most of these Godrej cupboards – almost every home if you were middle-class or over having one – if you were to unlock the safe and peek inside, you would most likely see the family gold, however modest; perhaps the family silver; almost certainly a wad of cash, however slim; some papers of identity confirming yes our family legally exists, we were born and here's the stamp to prove it; even passports for the more travelled and privileged. The safe was the place for Things of Value.

If we were to open Ferangiz's safe – though such an act would never be permissible or even thinkable

– but if we were to open it nonetheless and peer into its dark interior, we would see none of these things. We would simply see two piles of envelopes, left and right. The one to the left older, a tied pile of once-thumbed letters, tear-stained and worn, the aged paper now browned around the edges and spider-veined, the old envelopes that contained them bearing an ancient Lucknow postmark and the ardent hand of an army officer by the name of Homi Indrani, and addressed not to Ferangiz Mistry, no, to Izzy Mistry. The other pile to its right was higher – considerably higher – and newer, made yet more so by the fact that none of these letters, not one of them, had been opened. And each of these, bearing the New Delhi postmark were addressed in an untidy scrawl, not to Ferangiz Aunty, no, to Izzy Aunty.

But wait. Before we close the safe, if we were to put our heads or hands all the way in – this being an almost sacrilegious act, but since we are breaking bounds lets go all the way – tucked all the way at the back lay an old muslin drawstring bag, the still gold strings in a loose knot not unfastened for decades. If we were to reach in and pick it up, we would find it to have a certain weight, a certain timbre, and even as we hold it in our palm wondering what lies within, we somehow cannot untie it sensing it's a step too far, and we return it to the back of the cupboard setting it down gently in the exact position we found it all the way in the depths of the interior, the strings settling once more on the old safe shelf.

It was in front of this almirah that Ferangiz now stood, shaking with emotion. Her key turned in the lock and then opening the door, turning the lock of the inner safe too, she shoved in unopened the large flat brown envelope, that did not sit neatly on either pile but unevenly straddled them both; the large, flat, brown envelope that Farida had triumphantly delivered over the dining table at dinner saying, 'Mehnaz sent you this.'

Ferangiz had stiffened at the sight of the package, then had taken the envelope and lain it on the table beside her plate continuing to eat in her customary thick silence. Farida waited for her to say something but when nothing was forthcoming, she just couldn't contain herself. This was *her* moment, and she was going to take it. She wasn't going to let Ferangiz ignore it and pretend it didn't exist. In a voice that came out shrill and high, she said 'Aren't you going to open it?'

Again, Ferangiz did not respond. There was a stone-walled silence into which no one else around the table dared speak. After some seconds that felt like minutes had passed, Farida shrilled again 'It's her certificate. She did it Ferangiz. She did it. You said she couldn't, you said it wouldn't work and it has. She's an M.D, Ferangiz, she's done it!' Farida realized she was shrieking, and she stopped. Ferangiz simply stood up to leave the table leaving the envelope by her plate, while Farida shouted after her 'There's a picture of her baby Diya in there too! Don't you at least want to see that! Or don't you want to admit that she's a happy mother and a happy wife!' But Ferangiz was already striding back to her verandah, marching inside her darkened quarters. After some moments, as she stood there shimmering with anger and a million other emotions, there was a rustling under the door, and through the gap came first the corner and then the whole of the large brown envelope, entering Ferangiz's room like a flat accusation on the cold tiled floor.

The next morning while she took her tea on the verandah looking out over the orchard before she left for school, Ferangiz watched Farida going to the gate to collect the morning milk, Ferangiz thinking how like a coot she looked, her head hurrying before her, bobbing forward and back, her little body scurrying behind.

'Hema,' she said in earshot of her sister as she left for the day, 'I'll take my dinner on my verandah from now on,' turning to Farida as she headed out saying, 'give it four more years.'

CHAPTER 7

'Sit still!' Mehnaz cajoled Diya who was wriggling next to her, her face turned towards the open car window all the smells and soot of Delhi pouring in. Mehnaz

248

plaited her hair while she wiggled, into two stout pigtails that stuck out from either side of her head like handlebars revved and ready to go. She snapped the elastic bands on to the two ends and tied the white school ribbon into a bow on each, the handlebars now fluttering with two joyriding butterflies. Diya's nose stuck out into the Delhi air and into her day.

'We have to start getting up earlier, Diya!' said Mehnaz as she looked at her face in the driver's mirror from the back seat. She was still awkward about having a chauffeur, finding it uncomfortable that Bhupinder in his white liveried uniform and proud Sikh turban should have to drive her through her day. He however was devoted to his new madam maybe because she did not behave like one, she catching his eye in the mirror and both of them looking quickly away for different reasons, checking her own face best she could in the reflection of her window and adjusting her hurriedly tied sari.

'Come here,' she said, drawing Diya towards her for a quick cuddle, Diya squirming protestingly as they drew up at her pre-school. Diya skipped out, Mehnaz hurrying to keep up with her, carrying her little bright green hard plastic school case with tinsel stuck on. 'Bye kaleja, be a good girl!' but Diya was already off clambering over the climbing frame with her friends, shouting and squealing.

'How can you call her kaleja,' Manoj would say, 'such an ugly endearment! I would never want to be called someone's *liver*!'

'Izzy Aunty used to call me that and I loved it!' said Mehnaz. 'It was her way of saying there was only one of me, only one, irreplaceable and essential!'

'Not *that* essential to her'

He'd do that every now and again – probably more often than she cared to realize – make a mean remark like that. Mehnaz would try not to be hurt, attempting to take the bile out of it, 'Manoj, don't be mean! Anyway, you are my kaleja too. And my sweetheart.' And she'd wrap her arms around him. 'I'm late for my flight!' he'd say and move away.

The signs are always there, always there, it's just whether we choose to see them. We have seen them for her, we have seen many, many that Mehnaz has not yet seen and may never know of. When she allowed herself to notice the ones like this, she would frown slightly, feel her heart clutch, but then she would shake it away, put it down to his hard day, his bad mood, his tough case, his tiredness. She would brush it under the carpet, their red carpet under which there was not enough dust yet to make it look lumpy or trip them up.

Dressing unselfconsciously in their bedroom, wrapping her sari round and tucking it into the petticoat around her waist she would occasionally catch him looking at her, or perhaps more specifically looking at the extra layer that had gathered since having Diya, and she would catch a turn to his mouth that she wished she hadn't seen and she would dim a little and her skin would shrink. Or, that time they were getting ready to go to one of his dinner parties and she put on a pair of palazzo pants she had had tailored along with a cream silk top, and he said, 'What on earth are you wearing, you look like a brocaded elephant in that get-up,' and she'd changed into a sari instead. She brushed it under the carpet, I do need to lose some weight, she'd say to herself.

But it was hard not to notice that they fucked a lot less. There's always a point that couples fuck less and certainly having a baby girl and two demanding jobs doesn't ravish sexual appetites. Mehnaz knew that. Some days she was so tired after a long session in the clinic and taking care of Diya on either side of that, that the last thing she wanted was to roll about in the hay. But she wanted *him* to want to. It wasn't even the sex actually; it was the *contact.* She couldn't help notice that when he got home after work on the days he wasn't away – he was away so much – he was perfunctory in his contact. That was it, perfunctory. When they fell into bed at the end of the day, Diya sleeping at last in her own room next door, the cases done, the patients seen, in that day-done tiredness it was increasingly her hand that would reach for his and he would increasingly just turn over. No goodnight kiss.

251

It's not to say that they didn't. They did. Mostly in the morning, when he would wake up erect and his hand would reach for her then, reach out and in between her legs and she would murmur and say, 'Manoj I need to be up for Diya!' And he would say, 'Just a quick one baby…' He only called her baby when he wanted something, she tried not to notice that too. Perfunctory. This is what happens when you have children and busy jobs, she'd say to herself. But what of tenderness? Of concern? A goodnight kiss? She felt the lack of cherishment, trying not to notice, trying not to notice. She'd shower Diya with all her love and try not to notice.

Sometimes he'd come home like a randy dog. There was no stopping him then. It was usually after he'd been away or he'd won a case or sometimes both, but he would insist upon her, insist himself upon her, 'Come here baby,' he'd say and it would feel like those early days, when he would devour her, except she'd have this strange feeling that it wasn't her he was devouring. And when they'd finished and he'd get up or fall asleep next to her, Mehnaz would wonder why she felt so empty.

And she tried not to notice.

She missed home. She tried not to notice that too.

CHAPTER 8

With all things she tried not to notice, she didn't notice that the curl started to leave her hair, that the dewy plumpness of her skin grew dry, that the mischievous upturn of her mouth drooped slightly, that her toe-ring shone less and the sway of her bottom stilled. She didn't notice that she no longer sucked on mangoes in the thirsty way she used to, juice running down the sides of her mouth in a way that Manoj used to find erotic, licking it off her. 'Do you have to do that?' he'd say now, his lip curling. She didn't see that the clothes she picked to wear had changed from the silky parrot greens and peaches and blues to sober cotton prints. Besides, she was wrapped up with the clinic.

She had grown into an exceptional paediatrician. There were waiting lists, and in this unbeknownst to each other, she and her aunt were tied. If you had a baby or a little one of any shape or size and had ever taken them to the doctors, and if that doctor had been Mehnaz with her quality of tender, astute attention, you would never want to see any other doctor again. Her fingers would circle the measles bumps without fear, or stroke a forehead, her eyes would softly scan, her ears would take in the mummy's worried report or the daddy's one, and her hand would lay as much on their arms as the child's as she would say in a voice that made all worries ebb away, a voice that let you know that all would be well, a voice that gently but firmly gave you instructions, 'Mrs. Singh, your Balvir will be just fine, he's a fine little fighter, aren't you Balvir? Now be sure to give him these antibiotics three times a day for seven days. Complete the course. It's really important to complete the course. Balvir, you'll remind your mummy of that won't you? Lots of water, add a bit of honey to it if you like, lots of rest, dry toast and a little scrambled egg, do you like eggs beta? I thought you would! Little fighters love eggs.' The thing is Mehnaz didn't know how *not* to love. And here in this clinic her hair would curl and spring again. Love is like water. We crinkle up without it.

It wasn't just her bedside manner, though she knew just how much that counted for – our bodies and souls responding when they are spoken to the right way – she also had a sixth sense. The eczema covered little girl, seven years old, with raw peeling skin, eyes thin red slits, and the frightened-looking mother sitting behind her…something would make her ask, 'Is all well at home, Mrs. Sen?' And Mrs. Sen looking down and nodding, unable to look up.

'You can leave you know, you can leave. No one has to stay.' She'd say it so kindly and fiercely; the mother's shoulders then racking in fearful sobs.

'We have a spare bedroom at home. You can stay while you make arrangements.' The words were out, just like that, Manoj would go mad, she knew that, but sometimes she just didn't care.

254

'Are you out of your mind? We are not a charity!!' he said, when she arrived home with them. But in this Mehnaz was immovable.

'It's only for a couple of days Manoj, I cannot stand by knowing someone is being harmed.'

'We'll have a law case on our hands, do you think the husband is just going to roll over. We can't get involved in this!'

'He doesn't know where they are. Besides she's in the perfect household then, given that it's occupied by the country's most glittering lawyer,' her voice sharp.

And she would get on the phone to the women's safe houses and stay on there for hours, making arrangements for a return to eventual safety.

This is how it was. Sometimes she'd still be at work when Diya's school finished and Bhupinder would go to pick Diya up and bring her to the clinic, and Diya would play outside in the shade of the mango trees with Bhupinder watching over her while her mother administered and tended and reassured and diagnosed and saved.

Once, when the monsoon came late, the ground so parched, the mango leaves dry, dust coating everything thickly, the birds too thirsty to fly, the rain came suddenly and wildly in. Mehnaz ran out of the clinic the way everyone does when the rains arrive, to feel it and smell it and soak in it, only to see Diya picking her way carefully across the compound towards her, in a kind of tentative hopscotch, her eyes trained on the ground. Mehnaz's head tilted watching her from a distance. Diya was certainly not the kind of child to avoid puddles, what *was* she doing? Then it dawned on her. She was avoiding the earthworms, trying not to step on the zigzagging spaghetti that the rain had sprung! Mehnaz waited for her to stepstone across, bundling her into her arms when she reached her, loving her more than it was possible to love her, her heart aflood, their faces drenched in the pouring rain.

CHAPTER 9

Between Mehnaz and Diya much to Manoj's appre-hensible displeasure they were always bringing home waifs and strays. Diya came beaming in after school one day, a wriggling bulge in her skirt pocket, as she reached in and carefully pulled out a baby squirrel holding it gingerly in her hands, 'He had fallen out of the tree mama!' she whispered looking proudly at her mother.

'Did you wait to see if it's mummy would come?'

'Yes, he was alone and frightened! Can we keep him mama, can we keep him, I've named him Rajesh!'

'Daddy's not going to be very happy if there's a squirrel at the dining table, Diya. C'mon let's make it a little nest with a net cover for him and we can keep

Rajesh in your bedroom and then we'll call the vets and see what the best thing is to do ok?'

Manoj put his foot down when she came home with a baby goat. 'Diya, this house is not a zoo'! he shouted. 'And you encourage her Mehnaz, bringing orphans and battered wives back home every two minutes. I've had enough of it.' And Mehnaz would cajole him playfully or curl herself around him to placate him, but he would shake her off and angrily fix himself a whisky, till the day came when she didn't try to curl around him anymore.

The truth was there was always someone – four legged or two – being sheltered or fed or shielded or tended or hutched, and Mehnaz sympathized with him knowing it would test the patience of most, but he was hardly ever there and besides she just couldn't turn a blind eye to someone in trouble and neither it seemed could Diya. Consequently, it also wasn't unusual for the phone to ring and the caller to remain silent or disconnect when it was answered, as there was often a fugitive of some kind being temporarily housed in their midst. That's what Mehnaz put it down to, though she did find it odd how they got the number or didn't say anything having found it. 'Don't worry,' she'd say when the frightened woman looked at her in alarm, 'it was no one.' It didn't really occur to her to think otherwise, although sometimes the phone would ring in the middle of the night and Manoj would jump out of his skin a little more than was necessary and pick up the phone and put it straight down again with a curse and Mehnaz would apologise, saying 'Thank you baby for being ok with these calls,' and they'd go back to sleep.

He'd started coming home later and later, even when he was in town. 'It would be nice if Diya could see more of you, she misses you Manoj,' she'd say, and this was code for her missing him too. She'd say it to him sometimes, 'I miss you.'

'You know I'm busy with work, Mehnaz.'

And she'd feel that clutch in her heart.

Was this just what happened in marriages?

But despite the calls of logic and reason, every time a little more of her dimmed. And still that phone rang. Every now and again. In the middle of the night.

As Mehnaz was to discover there's two kinds of battering. There's the more obvious kind, the one concealed under an over-long sari sleeve, a purple eye behind dark shades, the one given away by a jolt or a cower at a loud noise or a raised voice, the one spoken in a tremble of a hand. Mehnaz knew that kind as it appeared every now and again in her clinic, appearing in a small woman behind a small child whom – horror of horrors – may also display the same tell-tale symptoms.

Then there's the other. The cuffs and blows that arrive in the form of a derision, an overlong absence, a curled mouth, a loveless fuck, a snipe or a sarcasm or a neglect. The bruises that stay when those knocks and digs and pokes hit the same spot over and over again in too quick succession to ever fully heal, or to no longer not notice. The hairline fractures that form when skin and soul are not upheld or sanctified or cherished. The slow, insidious poisoning that one has to be perfect to be loved, to not shit, or vomit, or get fat or tired, or have a birthmark, or save a desperate person who doesn't smell as fragrant as the candles in your home.

In the end, it was not the woman's voice she heard on the other end of the phone in the middle of the night while Manoj was away, a woman who quickly hung up but only after she'd said, 'Hello is Manoj there?' the loud ring waking up Diya who was asleep in Mehnaz's bed, saying 'Who is that mama, is it daddy?' And Mehnaz drawing her into her so close, so close, saying, 'No baby, it wasn't daddy.' And Diya saying, 'Mama you're holding me too tight, Rajesh will get squashed!' Mehnaz forgetting the squirrel that slept in the little pouch tied on to her daughter's pyjamas.

In the end it was the rain that ended it all.

Or maybe it was the heavens.

CHAPTER 10

There's always the thing, the final thing, the thing that turns the tide. Despite the signals or the gathering storm or all the signs not noticed, despite all that has been compromised, rationalised, excused, ignored, lived with and longed for, despite all the emotional blows and bruises endured, there's always one moment that changes everything. We never know it's coming, we never do, but when it does, it comes in so fast and without warning, it's almost like it's been there all along. Yes, almost like it's been there all along. And there in a seeming instant everything is changed, evermore.

The monsoon swept in again the following year, like it did most every year, its arrival across the skies bringing relief not only for the farmers – the rains if they failed being a disaster of a calamitous scale – but from the scalding summer air, as well the holy reassurance of the seasons. Mehnaz and Diya had got soaked to the skin running in from the car to the house and they both showered, hot showers, coming out hair wet, eyes shining into the washed world, having hot tea and biscuits on the verandah, just in time to see Manoj get out of his office car and come through the gate.

'Daddy!' shouted Diya, thrilled to see her father.

But Manoj appeared in a thunderous mood. He marched across the compound towards the house in a seemingly silent rage.

Diya shouted again, 'Daddy! Be careful of the earthworms!'

Manoj looked at Diya, right at her, and then almost as if time stalled to mark it, he lifted his foot high in slow motion, and his leather-soled size 11 handmade shoe came crunching down. He turned his foot this way, then that, the gritty mud grinding and squelching, making sure that even a resourceful double-ended hermaphrodite would not recover.

And there. Just like that, for Mehnaz, it was over.

In the end, it was the rain that ended it all.

Or maybe it was the heavens.

CHAPTER 11

Manoj would say later to her that he'd been in an atrocious mood. A terrible mood. He'd lost his case, a big case, a very, very important, very high-profile case. His reputation was on the line. He'd been angry and very upset.

But it was no good.

The worm had turned.

She didn't even ask him about Priti.

They settled out of court. He'd threatened her with destitution. 'If you want to leave, LEAVE. Just GO.' He'd threatened her with humiliation. 'I must be the first man on earth whose wife's ground for divorce is standing on a worm.' He'd threatened her with his might. 'You think you can take *me* on in a lawsuit?'

She said, I'll take you on.

And the way she said it, he knew that she knew.

She said, 'This is not my life. I want to be cherished. I want Diya to be cherished.'

And he saw again in that moment the mother-maiden he had forgotten how to see.

The thing about Persian tapestries is we never own them, they are not ours to own even though we might think they are, all we must do is cherish them, look after them, so they keep their natural shine.

She didn't take him to the cleaners, though she could have. She asked for a small apartment in south Delhi for herself and Diya. 'She needs a park she can play in, a colony with lots of other kids and it needs to be safe. That's all. I don't want any alimony.'

'Don't you want to run back to Poona? To your amazing aunt?' The familiar curve to his mouth was back now he knew he couldn't win.

She didn't. Not yet anyway. Mehnaz had not been back since that visit for Almaz's sixteenth birthday 5 years ago. Izzy Aunty had not spoken or written to her once since she had left, and she couldn't bear the thought of another icy reception. Besides the clinic was here. Diya's school was here. She needed to gather herself, work out what she wanted to do. Get back to herself.

The rain had returned her curls to full force, and hand in hand with her little girl – whom he had not fought for custody of – the spring returned to her step. Maybe it's not so much that we need to be loved. Just that we need not to *not be*.

Other than custody, the one thing they did easily agree on was to keep the families out of it. Mehnaz did not want her mother worrying and Manoj did not want his mother's hysteria. They decided to tell them only when the divorce was signed and sealed, and she and Diya had moved out.

'Ma, I have something to tell you…' Mehnaz calling her from the small living room of the new apartment.

'Manoj and I have split up'

There was a long silence at the other end, her mother not saying anything. Almost as if her mother had been expecting the news. Yes, almost as if her mother had been expecting the news, all along.

CHAPTER 12

Farida didn't actually tell Ferangiz the news. She couldn't stand the thought of it. She couldn't stand the thought of Ferangiz's I-was-right-I-told-you-I-was-right-but-I'm-not-going-to-say-it-because-you-know-it-and-I-always-knew-it look on her face. Maybe she'd heard through Shanaz or Almaz or Hema or through the endless vine of people that hung around her verandah these days, cloying around her, clutching on to her every astrological word. Wherever she had heard from, Farida knew immediately when she had. She knew because as she watched her sister go to the gate to collect her newspaper the next morning, Ferangiz's head was a little higher, her step though it could never be described as springy just a little bit more righteous, and then as she reached for the paper, turned and came back, for a moment – just a moment – their eyes met, and there was a hint, a tiny upturn of victory in her thin-lipped mouth. Farida thought how like an old heron her sister looked, tall, grey, pointy and superior, holding her paper like a fresh caught fish as she storked triumphantly across the yard back to her solitary pond.

CHAPTER 13

Days and days and months and months and years and years passed, everyone lost count if they were counting at all, maybe it was long and maybe it was not long at all, one day looking like the next, a flurry of endeavour and hope and regret. When we arrive in the moment we're about to witness, Mehnaz was 29 years old, and a full ten years had passed since she had left Balthazar House all that time ago. She went about her business of single-handedly raising Diya and Diya's menagerie, Manoj dropping in every now and again with guilt gilded gifts for his daughter but not much else, Mehnaz making sure she was out when he did, the reports, now that she had left him, of his many indiscretions having reached her ears.

Let's not pretend it was easy. It wasn't. Her hands were full, the days were hot, unimaginably hot, Diya could be a handful, and her spirit and bank balance sometimes teetered. She tended unceasingly to all those whose little chests coughed and noses sneezed and skin shivered as well as those whose hearts quivered, in the ever-crowded ever-queueing waiting room outside her clinic door. No one yet had taken residence in her heart or bed and her sweet, plump, day-spent body fell asleep at night alone, her curly hair fanning around her head un-stroked, though come to think of it Manoj had never stroked it anyway.

Some people seemed to think that a divorced woman was fair game, anybody's bacon, and she had to fend off a fair few foistings including a recurring attempt by her corpulent married neighbour. But mainly she was encircled by friends and patients who guarded her rather fiercely – a little too fiercely perhaps – or who trotted in smitten suitors of varying shapes and sizes while pretending they were doing no such thing. The fact was, despite Manoj turning out to be the worm he was, no one had touched her in the same way since, and she was in no hurry to be similarly touched.

Her mother worried. But that's what mothers do, Mehnaz knew that now. This time, other than regular phone-calls to check on her, Farida did not try to matchmake though she did regularly ask her daughter to come back to Poona. 'I can help you here Mehnu, you can open your clinic here, the Poona schools are so much nicer than those Delhi ones, come home, Mehnu.' And Mehnaz would feel the familiar pang at the sound of the word…Poona…and an even deeper one at the sound of the word home. 'No ma,' she'd say, 'Delhi is home now,' both of them knowing though neither said it why Mehnaz would not return.

Not a word from Izzy Aunty.

Not one single word.

Not one.

And so after days and days and months and months and years and years, maybe it was long and maybe it was not long at all, we arrive in the moment we are about to witness, when Mehnaz and Diya got home, crashing into the house after the dusty day, Mehnaz telling Diya about the little patient she'd just seen who's nose had been pecked by a hawk, 'So don't eat your sandwiches in the playground Diya.' and Diya's eye's widening saying, 'Has she got no nose now mummy?!' when the phone-rang, Diya running to pick it up as she always did, 'Hello, this is Diya's residence.'

'Hello granny, a hawk pecked a girl's nose!'

But she didn't chatter as usual, saying 'Yes, Granny, she's here,' and passed the phone to her mother.

Farida, unusually, cut straight to it.

'Mehnaz, Ferangiz Aunty isn't eating'

'What do you mean, ma?'

'Hema said she just suddenly stopped. She takes her her breakfast and dinner, but she doesn't eat it. Hema comes back to clear it up and it's on the table untouched.'

'When did this start?'

'Two or three days ago, I think?'

'Two or three days! Oh my goodness. How is she feeling?'

'You know she doesn't speak to me, Mehnu.'

'You'll have to speak to her, Ma. That's not right for her to suddenly lose her appetite completely. Have you called Dr Wadia?'

'I can't do that without speaking to her first. You know what she's like.'

'Yes, you can. Go and talk to her, see how she is, maybe it's just a tummy bug, and then if it continues call the doctor ok? And make sure she has lots of fluids.'

CHAPTER 14

The trouble was no one could make Ferangiz have lots of fluids. She had taken to her bed, lying on her back in the darkened room, looking disconcertingly corpse-like almost as if swathed ready for burial in her handloom sari, hair neatly plaited, her long, white feet pointing towards the ceiling. That's the impression she made on Farida at any rate as she tentatively knocked, and then when Ferangiz didn't answer, opened the door and stepped into the darkened room, seeing Ferangiz lying on her bed in the corner. Ferangiz's original mahogany bed had finally given way some years ago, woodworm worming its way undetected through the posts and struts till Ferangiz found herself wobbling every time she turned over in her sleep, the carpenter proclaiming her only one woodworm nibble away from being deposited on the floor. Ferangiz replaced it with a charpoy bed.

Farida remembered the charpoy being delivered, watching it arriving with horror, we are not the sort of family who sleeps on charpoys, what would mummy think of this! However the fact was that despite the tuition pupils and fortune seekers who attended her verandah, Ferangiz never took more than a token sum for her services and the family still subsisted on Anosh's pension as well as Ferangiz's meagre one from the school, and the driveway of Balthazar House was far from paved with gold. Admittedly buying a new solid wood bed would have been a stretch, but a charpoy! Did her sister always have to take things to such extremes? Nothing signified shame more to Farida than that bed arriving, and even now as she entered Ferangiz's room she flinched at the sight of it, even before fully apprehending the state of her sister, utterly dismayed by the skeletal form she saw.

'Ferangiz, what's wrong?!' she said, rushing over to the charpoy all the years of cold war forgotten.

Ferangiz's voice came out thin and weak.

'Nothing, I've just lost my appetite. Leave me be.'

'Hema told me you haven't eaten since Monday. That's almost three days!'

'I know. I don't want to eat, Farida. Just leave me please.'

'I've brought you a bowl of kanji, just have a spoon or two of that'

'I don't want any'

'I'm going to call the doctor, Ferangiz'

'No! I don't want the doctor. Stop fussing please, Farida. It will pass.'

'But you look terribly weak. Have a spoonful of kanji, or I will have to call the doctor.' Farida was bending over her with the bowl of the clear, nutritious gruel, the closest contact the two sisters had ever been in since they were little girls.

'If you do that I will never forgive you, Farida. Just leave the bowl, I'll have it.'

'Will you promise?'

'Just leave the bowl.'

'I'll come and check on you in a couple of hours ok?'

Ferangiz didn't reply.

When Farida returned once again just as night fell, stepping into the otherwise forbidden anteroom of Ferangiz's chambers where she now lay in the dark,

Farida making her way over to the bed, unfamiliarly seeking out the light switch that lit the green lamp by her bedside, next to which the kanji lay untouched.

Ferangiz's eyes were closed and the room was so silent, so very still, that Farida's own heart almost stopped. Very slowly, very tentatively she lay her hand on her sister's shoulder, and out of her mouth came a word she didn't expect. 'Didi?' she said, the word for sister that she used to call her when she was very small, way back then before dada had died. 'Didi?'

Ferangiz stirred and Farida let out a relieved sigh, though the relief didn't last for long. Her sister's skin had visibly sunk even in those short hours. She reached for a glass in a panic – she should have called the doctor earlier – and shook her sister gently.

'Ferangiz have some water, you have to have some water at least!'

Nothing.

'Ferangiz sit up a bit and have this.'

'I have to go to the toilet,' said Ferangiz eventually, slowly moving to get to her feet and to her own surprise falling backwards on to the bed. Farida came forward to help her, but she weakly shook her off and forced herself, forced herself with all the determination that was left in her to make it to the bathroom. Farida waited, scared to ask if she needed help, as much as not to.

After what seemed like an age Ferangiz made it back, sitting on the edge of the charpoy to recover, leaning forward, beads of sweat from the effort gathering on her brow.

'Please have some water Ferangiz, otherwise I'm calling the doctor right now.'

Ferangiz took the glass, her hands unsteady. Slowly she took a sip. She held the water in her mouth, careful not to swallow. She must not swallow. She *will not* swallow. Her eyes hardened in determination and in that tightening a soft, salty, tear escaped, slipping down her cheek and coming to rest in the dry shelf of her lower lip. She must not lick it, she *will not* lick it, no water will pass her lips.

She looked at Farida. And spat the water out at her feet.

CHAPTER 15

'She did what?' Mehnaz was unsure whether she was more shocked by the spitting or her mother's bleak description of her aunt's condition.

'She's very weak. I think she's dying, Mehnu!' her mother cried.

How had this happened so quickly? Where had this illness come from suddenly and without warning?

The doctor part of her took over.

'Ok ma, calm down, take a breath I need you to talk me through this properly ok?'

'Ok.'

'So Hema said Izzy Aunty stopped eating on Sunday night?'

Mehnaz looked out of professional habit at the calendar on the wall, Sunday 27th December. Something in her fluttered as her eyes rested on the date, she couldn't really say what, and she frowned.

'Yes, she didn't eat her Sunday night dinner.'

'She had breakfast that day?'

'Yes, that's what Hema said. She had akuri. In fact Hema said she requested that especially that morning and she had seconds, which she never does as you know.'

Mehnaz knew. Mehnaz also knew that akuri was her aunt's favourite meal.

'Ok, and then what happened?'

'She saw all her tuition students and astrology people as usual.'

'So she worked all day Sunday?'

'To the best of my knowledge, yes. She works seven days a week, Mehnu. When I went out that afternoon to meet Sapna for Sunday tea, Mr. Joshi was there checking all those waiting people in, you know he's her full-time secretary now.'

'No, I didn't, and I didn't know that she had queues. Let's stick to the important facts, ma. So she had a full breakfast and a full working day. Did she have her tea at 5pm?'

'Yes Mehnu, she had it just as usual, like she always does.'

'Then Hema, took her dinner?'

'That's what Hema told me.'

'And she left it untouched?'

'Yes.'

'And since then, where are we now, Wednesday night, she has not eaten?'

'Yes,' said her mother 'Hema said that she assumed she was not hungry. She just serves the dinner on the verandah, she didn't realise she was laid up in bed, that's why she only told me today.'

'The problem is everyone is too damn scared of Izzy Aunty, Hema should have told you earlier! You should have told me earlier!'

'I know Mehnu, I'm sorry.'

'Ok, so she went from perfectly fine, a full working day and a healthier than normal appetite to this. She's not vomiting, not complaining of headaches, not got a fever?'

'She's not complaining of anything, but she's refusing any food and even water.'

'She's not had *any water*?!'

Mehnaz took a breath, her stomach sick, her mind scrambling.

'Something is very wrong Ma, get Dr Wadia to come now if he can or if not very first thing tomorrow.

I'm going to catch the early flight tomorrow morning. I'll bring Diya with me. If I catch the 6 am flight, I'll be home by 9.30 am.'

'Oh thank God, Mehnu, I can't handle this by myself!'

'I know ma.'

'Oh, and ma? Have Hema sleep in Izzy Aunty's room tonight, or if she won't allow it then get Raju to make a bed for Hema outside her bedroom door. And call me immediately if anything changes.'

CHAPTER 16

Mehnaz put the phone down slowly. She sank into the faded sofa, striped light and dark by the streetlights through the blinds, her hand over her mouth, keeping the shock in. Was Izzy Aunty dying? She felt faint.

She sat there for a good while, trying to take it in, mentally scanning her medical cornucopias for a potential diagnosis. The ceiling fan turned above, slicing the air, whish, whosh, making the cheap, thin pages of the wall calendar flutter. Mehnaz's eyes once more flickered over that date – 27 December, what was that? Why was it ringing a bell? Had she forgotten someone? To do something? Her memory clawed, but no, she couldn't reach it.

It was enough to make herself move and she rose, starting to pack, a few of Diya's dresses, a few saris and salwars, she'd have to ask the clinic to come and get Rajesh, Diya would kick up a fuss about that, but squirrels wouldn't exactly be welcome on planes. She finally sat on the edge of the bed, lying down eventually to neither sleep nor dream, the alarm set for 4 am. She'd called Bhupinder her old driver, ever there for her in an emergency despite no longer being in her employ, and he was coming before his working day began to take them to the airport.

The morning was a blur, Diya confused, full of questions about this other granny whom she'd never met and tearful about leaving Rajesh without warning. But they managed to bundle into the car, Bhupinder speeding them to the airport.

It was only when the plane started to taxi and finally lift off towards Poona, Mehnaz bursting into tears just as Rajesh popped out of the top of Diya's shirt, it was only then that she realized she'd said she was coming *home*.

Diya thought she was upset about her sneaking in the squirrel.

Part Seven

THE RETURN PRESENT

CHAPTER 1

Whatever Mehnaz had expected on arriving at Balthazar House – which was not very much, most of her mental energy going into churning over in her mind what this illness could be, scanning through her now considerable clinical experience for what could have brought it on so suddenly, as well as fielding Diya's questions and holding her own many turbulent emotions at bay – whatever she had expected, it was not what she saw.

Outside the gate was a silent sea of people. There was such a crowd that the taxi could barely approach and Mehnaz and Diya had to get out while the taxi driver lugged their bags.

Holding tightly to Diya's hands, Mehnaz pushed her way through the crowd, her heart doing strange things when she saw the gate she knew so well, now even more rusty with a few makeshift panels hammered in to patch up corrosion. My goodness, this is what mama must have meant when she said there were queues these days for Izzy Aunty! But don't they know she's sick?

'Please stand outside ma'am,' said a tall elderly gentleman standing guard just inside the small inset gate.

'Excuse me, I live here' she said feeling a rush of anger.

'Sorry, ma'am. Your good name?'

'I'm Miss Mistry's niece,' she said stepping over the threshold with Diya without waiting for his permission, 'you must be Mr Joshi?'

'Yes, ma'am, I am.'

'Why are these people here? Don't they know she's ill?'

Mr. Joshi shut the gate behind her and the calm and shade of Balthazar descended on them.

'No ma'am,' he said 'they are not waiting to see her. Miss Mistry has no appointments in her diary. She works so hard, ma'am. She finally said she was going to have a long rest and told me not to take any bookings after 27 December. But instead, she has fallen ill! These are all people who she has helped, who are worried. That's why I came, because I heard there was crowd here, and Ms. Farida was getting upset…'

His voice trailed away. Mehnaz was looking at him in shock.

'Mr. Joshi, when did Miss Mistry tell you to stop taking appointments?'

'Oh, long time ago ma'am, maybe 9-10 months back, she has a long waiting list ma'am, so it has to be planned in advance. She doesn't like to let people down, ma'am.'

When pennies drop, they all drop at once, like a winning slot machine, all the mechanics moving and whirring, releasing the banks of memory, and connections crashing in one after the other into the tray.

Mehnaz was looking at him but not looking at him. *27 December 1998*. That was the date on the piece of paper that Izzy Aunty had given her to hand to her mother all those years ago!

Her sixth sense had done it again.

Oh my God, she thought, Izzy Aunty was predicting the date of her own death on that note! And when it didn't happen, when it didn't happen, she stopped eating and drinking that very night, oh my God…Izzy Aunty is starving herself to death! Oh my God, she thought, oh my God, she doesn't want to admit to mama she was wrong. She would rather die!'

The last penny hit the tray with a solid clunk, a clunk that slotted right into place and Mehnaz knew with absolute conviction, no doubt, no doubt at all, so sure she would stake her own and Diya's lives on it, that she was right. Just then, just as the last penny hit soundly home, her mother appeared on the porch and Diya went running off to greet her.

'Does she know I'm here, Ma?'

'No, we didn't tell her in case it disturbed her. We just wanted you to get here Mehnu.'

'Good, I'm glad. Has Dr Wadia been?'

'He's coming right now. Hema is keeping watch outside her door; she wouldn't let her sleep in the room.'

'Ok, I'm just going to go the kitchen to make her a cup of tea to take in with me, Diya be a good girl and stay with granny ok?'

Mehnaz walked into the kitchen, her hands following the familiar route they still knew so well. Everything was where it always was. Her fingers found the little latch, swinging open the door under the stove, reaching in for the little saucepan she used to boil the water, filling it and putting it on the gas. Then over to the cupboard to the right, the little steel canister, the one on the left with the orange pekoe for the morning. She shuffled through the cutlery holder, finding her spoon, one and a quarter, into the teapot, lifting the pan off the gas just before it came to the boil, pouring it in. She swirled it a couple of times, then found Izzy Aunty's cup and saucer, setting them all on the tray.

She took a breath. Then laying a hand on her heart and saying a prayer, God please let her listen, please let her stop this crazy starvation fast, please be with me, please be with us, she lifted the tray and walked, her feet knowing every crack and contour of the floor, towards Izzy Aunty's verandah.

Hema jumped up, as much as poor dear old Hema could jump, given she was so much older and so much heavier now, her oiled hair, white but still curly, giving the impression of a startled judge. Mehnaz's eyes held greeting and warning, unable to lift her fingers to her lips to signal to Hema to be quiet, but Hema miraculously interpreting the slight shake of Mehnaz's head exactly as it was meant. They would embrace later. Mehnaz signalled with her eyes for Hema to open Izzy Aunty's door so she could carry the tray through, which, thank goodness, she had not locked from the inside, and she stepped in.

It was morning, so the room had a dim dappled light, though still dark and shadowy. 'Who's that?' Izzy Aunty's voice, barely perceptible, still trying to be strident and failing, lying on her back, squinting towards the door, the watery sun just catching her eyes. Mehnaz's eyes quickly adjusted, Izzy Aunty's form, white, thin, ethereal in the shadows, shocking her deeply.

Mehnaz closed the door behind her with her foot, making her way quietly over, 'Izzy Aunty,' she whispered, so soft she could hardly hear herself, could hardly speak, 'Izzy Aunty, it's me.'

Ferangiz, squinted towards her, delirious and fading now on her third day without food or water.

'Mehnaz?'

'Yes, I brought you some tea.'

Mehnaz forced herself to retain her composure, acting as if she'd seen her yesterday, that it was teatime like any other day, instinctively knowing it was needed now more than ever. She set the tray down on the bedside table and pulled up a chair to sit beside her.

For a moment niece and aunt remained like that, Mehnaz looking down towards the floor, knowing the way she always knew what to do, that her aunt needed a moment to take her presence in, without the intrusion and force of eye contact.

'I don't want any tea,' Ferangiz said finally, her voice almost imperceptible.

Mehnaz's hand rested on the edge of the charpoy, trying not to notice how thin and old and frail her aunt looked, trying to keep her voice steady and the tears back.

'I've missed you so much, Izzy Aunty.'

And Ferangiz's head turned away.

'You were right, you were right about Manoj, Izzy Aunty. He was a cad. But I had to go through it, it was part of my life and it gave me my Diya. You were right, but you don't have to do this, Izzy Aunty. I'm home, you don't have to be right anymore.'

Ferangiz's head remained turned away and her body shook slightly.

Mehnaz sat holding back the tears, and then with the last of her composure, she said quietly, so quietly, 'Mama's forgotten all about that note, you know. She threw it away years ago.'

The air around them sharpened in recognition of what was being said.

'*Everything's* forgotten Izzy Aunty.'

And because life has a way of bringing us things we least expect at the moments we least expect them, and because too what may seem like a death may in fact be a birth, it being necessary to leave what we know behind to make way for what we *need* to arrive, it was Izzy Aunty's hand that closed tightly over Mehnaz's, Izzy Aunty's hand that had not held

284

another since Homi had died and whose lips had never, not once, uttered a word of apology, it was Izzy Aunty who turned her wet, withered face towards Mehnaz and whispered 'I'm so sorry for everything, kaleja.'

Mehnaz's head bent, resting her forehead on her aunt's tightly clasped hand, tears falling.

Just at that moment, because life has a way of bringing us things we least expect at the moments we least expect them, there was a knock on the door and Dr Wadia – not the old Dr Wadia whom Mehnaz was expecting, but the young Dr Wadia, Dr Zubin Wadia if we are to be exact – asked if he may come in.

It was about or exactly 9.46 am. This time there wasn't a clang of a gate, nor a trumpet horn, but the solid knock of warm wood, and a soft, kind burr at the bedside that said 'Ladies, is everything well?'

'Yes,' one said, so softly it was impossible to say whom, though to look at their tear-creased faces one might easily think otherwise, 'everything is very well indeed.'

Epilogue

EVEN LATER

The morning of the wedding, Diya was skittering around Ferangiz's room looking for some tinsel to put around Rajesh's neck, not knowing that Ferangiz's room was the last place one could expect to find tinsel. 'Are you sure you don't have any, Izzy Granny? I promised Zubin Uncle that Rajesh would look good for the ceremony.'

'Well, let me see,' said Izzy Granny.

She opened her almirah, and thence the inset safe for Things of Value, in which were two piles of letters, both opened. Her hand reached inside for the little muslin bag all the way to the back that was tied with a golden thread. She retrieved the bag and pulled the thread free, handing it to Diya, who gave a little whoop. 'This is perfect Izzy Granny!' Then she took the little girl's hand, the muslin bag in the other and walked through the flower laden Balthazar House that was all dressed up for the ceremony that morning, in search of Mehnaz, finding her in the kitchen in last minute preparation, bustling about with Farida, Hema and Almaz, while Shanaz fine-tuned her poetry reading at the dining table oblivious of everyone else, and Raju gave a final flourish to the yard with his broom.

There she stood, luminous in her Parsi wedding white, one finger tasting the paneer, the other offering Almaz the chicken, while Izzy Aunty tipped out of the muslin bag the sapphire necklace she was to wear to her own wedding – because Homi would always love blue – walking over to her niece and fastening the precious gems around her neck.

High, high above, Kalina, who we may have forgotten all about, but has certainly not forgotten us, did a great swoop and a whoop, her black feathers catching the light, all their iridescence shining in sapphires and emerald blues, such that to watch her anyone would think she was a kingfisher.

ABOUT THE AUTHOR

Sonia Lakshman grew up in India to an English mother and Indian father and an irreverent DNA, coming to live in the UK aged 19 where she has lived ever since. She started out working in the media, then sailed the stories of the soul as a career and leadership coach, now devoted to the mission for climate and nature – animals in particular. She prefers dogs to cats, dancing over debating, likes salad *and* chips. One of her favourite words is 'cosmos' – you have to agree it's a wondrous word. This is her first novel.

Sonialakshman.com

Dear Reader

*If you enjoyed my book, it would be lovely
if you could leave a review on Amazon.*

*And, if you know a literary agent or publisher who may find
it of interest, I'd hugely appreciate you passing it on or an
introduction. It's currently self-published.*

Thank you so much.

Printed in Dunstable, United Kingdom